TO DANCE
WITH THE WHITE DOG

TO DANCE
WITH THE WHITE DOG

A novel by

Terry Kay

PEACHTREE PUBLISHERS, LTD.
ATLANTA

Ω
Published by
PEACHTREE PUBLISHERS, LTD.
1700 Chattahoochee Avenue
Atlanta, Georgia 30318-2112

Manufactured in the United States of America

7th printing 2001

Library of Congress Cataloging in Publication Data

Kay, Terry.
    To dance with the white dog : a novel / by Terry Kay.
        p.   cm.
    ISBN 1-56145-002-2 (hardcover)
    I. Title
PS3561.A885T6   1990
  813'.54—dc20
90-41752
                                      CIP

This book is dedicated with love to my sisters and brothers —Lula, Jean, Sara, Nell, Betty, Toombs, Patsy, Peggy, John, and Gary — who saw the white dog dance; also, to the memory of our brother, Thomas, who has been for me the hero of wonderful legends which exist inexplicably, yet vividly, in my imagination.

ONE

He understood what they were thinking and saying: Old man that he is, what's to become of him? Let's talk it out, they were saying cautiously.

Let's talk it out and come up with some solution while we're here, all of us, and it's on our minds. See if we can approach him about it, reason with him even if the timing's bad.

Makes sense. Can't put it off forever, no matter how painful it'll be to say aloud.

I don't know. Not now. Can't we wait? Just a few days, maybe.

But he'll not make it being alone, not likely, not half- crippled as he is.

Not used to being alone, they were saying. Not at all.

That's true. That's true. Always been somebody else around, even with all of us taking our leave, one by one.

She was here. When we were all gone, at least she was here.

Yes, that's true. Won't be the same now, not at all, not without her. Something'll have to take up the slack.

What are we going to do? We can't say anything, not now.

Soon. We've got to, soon.

He'll be stubborn about it, whatever we think.

He's got pride, all right. It's his mark. Thinks he's still bull-strong, and it's sad.

Still that way in his mind — bull-strong.

They were saying these things about him and did not know that he understood them, that he knew what they were saying. They were whispering among themselves that an old man's mind plays tricks, that it feeds on the swill of illusion, like carnival shell games that are faster than the eye. They were saying it would be a great pity to see him that way.

It was now past midnight. They had arrived — his sons and daughters — in the afternoon and during the hours of the dark May evening, and they had embraced him and wept before him and then they had huddled around the large kitchen table to drink strong coffee and talk quietly among themselves in sad, worried voices.

They would not know it, but he understood what they were thinking and saying: Old man that he is, what's to become of him?

He sat alone in his padded rocker in the middle room, near his rolltop desk, his good leg propped on the bottom brace of his aluminum walker, his head against the pillowed headrest of the chair, his eyes closed. He was not asleep, but he pretended sleep. It was better that way. He wanted his sons and daughters to get it said. Maybe by saying it, they'd get over it and wouldn't hover over him as though he was an invalid.

He knew about hovering. He had been called home from Madison, from school, to care for his grandfather when he was seventeen and he'd hovered, watching his grandfather wither into death. He had not wanted to stay with his grandfather, but it was expected and he'd done it. He'd hovered, watching, watching. He did not want his children to be watching, watching.

They mean well enough, he thought. And they need to talk of something. They need to feel needed. They would not bicker, though. It was not the time or the place or the mood for bickering. Not now. Perhaps later, when they had stopped their pitying. And perhaps they should. They had tempers for it, each of them — temper and his pride (and hers). It would not be enough for any of them to give up an argument without their say. God knows, he thought, I've listened to them for more than fifty years, and they've never backed off without having their say. But they mean well, sitting there in the kitchen, drinking their strong coffee at the crowded table, talking of what would become of him.

The window beside his roll-top desk was open and he could smell the greening of spring and hear the squalling of swamp bugs, and clearer than the swamp bugs and the low, serious voices of his children from the kitchen, he could hear the sharp, spirited whistle of a whippoorwill below the barns. He opened his lips

2

slightly, moistened them, drew in a breath and soundlessly answered the whippoorwill. She had liked him answering birdcalls — the whippoorwill, the bobwhite. In spring and in summer, at dusk, they had often sat on the screened-in sideporch and listened to the birds, and he had answered them, cry for cry, and it had pleased her to hear him playful after a day of field work. Sometimes the bobwhites would walk into the grass of the lawn when he whistled for them and she would whisper, "Look!" She would not permit anyone to kill the bobwhites that lived in the grainfields of their land. The bobwhites were too trusting, too easy to call up for the gunsights of a hunter.

Because of her, he had learned to look for the birds — the darting flight of wild canaries (yellow sun on yellow wings), the chesty preening of redbirds and bluebirds, the blackbird with the red-tipped wings like startling epaulets. Often he had strewn grain over the ground outside the kitchen window so she could see the birds feeding as she worked.

The grass of the lawn had been cut earlier that day by one of the sons-in-law off work, and the smell of the cut grass, through the window beside the roll-top desk, was sweet as mint.

He reached for a letter on the desk. It was an invitation to a reunion for the classes of 1910-1915 at Madison Agricultural and Mechanical — Madison A&M. Sixty years, he thought. Sixty years. The invitation had arrived that day. She had said, "I want to go to this. It's been a long time since we went back." And he had taken the letter and put it away on his desk. He had said to her, "We'll see about it." He read the letter again in the dim light of the table lamp. It was signed by Martha Dunaway Kerr. He put the letter back on his desk and nestled his neck against the pillowed headrest and closed his eyes again.

He could hear the footsteps of someone — perhaps two people — entering the middle room from the kitchen, but he did not open his eyes. The footsteps stopped at the door. There was a pause of silence, and he knew he was being watched. Then he heard the soft, backward steps of retreat. He knew what was being said inside the kitchen: "He's sleeping." And he knew someone (one of the daughters, likely) answered: "Let him. He needs it."

Curious, he thought — knowing there was someone, perhaps two people, at the door leading into the room, knowing exactly where they were standing as they watched him, knowing they had walked back to the kitchen table. Or was it curious? No, he decided. No. It was his house. He knew it board by board, could hear the voices of its timbers and walk its walls in blind dark, reading its raised-lettered Braille with his fingertips.

He had walked the walls many times at night, going to her bed to see if she was sleeping, but he would not go to her bed this night. No, not this night.

He opened his eyes, felt them dampen. He moved his head on the headrest of the chair. He could feel the ache in his bad leg, in the thigh, in the hip that had been twice replaced with an artificial joint. One of his daughters (he could not remember which) had given him aspirin for the ache, but it had not helped. Tomorrow he would ask for something stronger from the druggist, something to numb the bruise deep in his hip, something pleasant to calm him, to keep him from reeling before the dizzying swarm of sons and daughters and grandsons and granddaughters and drawn-faced neighbors who would fill the house with their mumblings and their platters of food offerings. The druggist was wise enough to know what was needed. The druggist would know better than anyone.

The whippoorwill called again, but was farther away, deeper in the swamp.

He pulled his watch from his shirt pocket. The watch was tied by a cut-off shoestring that he had threaded through a buttonhole high on his shirt — a practice that annoyed his daughters because it made him appear unkempt. It was twelve-forty. It does not take long to die, he thought.

He stared at the face of the watch, at the dull lime green of the see-in-the-dark numbers and the long and the short hands, and he subtracted away the hours in his mind. Five? Almost six? He counted the hours again. Yes, almost six, he decided. It had happened quickly. He slipped the watch back into his shirt pocket and closed his eyes again. From the kitchen, he could hear the mewing of crying.

I, too, want to die as quickly, he thought.

She did not answer when he called (though he could no longer hear all voices well, he had trained his senses for her, knew her quietest words) and he pulled himself from the oversized armchair, up to the top brace of the aluminum walker, and dragged-walked from the living room to find her.

"What're you doing?" he said in a loud voice. "Thought you were coming back. Thought you wanted to see the show on the TV."

She did not answer, and he went from the middle room to the kitchen and then to the back bedroom. He saw her on the floor, near the bed, on her left side, and he knew immediately what had happened. He shoved his walker aside and tried to run to her, but could not and he hobbled, good leg, bad leg, leaning against the walls for support until he reached her. He touched her neck. He could feel a quivering pulse, a twitch of blood flow, but he could not feel her breathing, and he sank beside her on his good leg and turned her to him and slipped his arm beneath the cradle of her neck and pushed open her mouth with his fingers and closed his own mouth over hers and began to search for life with his tongue, but there was only the cooling taste of saliva. He kissed her gently.

"Don't," he said aloud. "Don't do this. Don't do this."

He knew he could not lift her and it angered him. Old damned body, he thought. Old damned body. He eased her head down and pulled his arm from beneath her neck and rolled awkwardly and caught the knob of the closet door near him and drew himself up from the floor. The telephone was in the hallway and he stumbled, good leg, bad leg, to it and dialed a number. Four hundred yards away, across the sidelawn and a road, a daughter answered.

"It's your mama," he said.

"Mama?" his daughter asked, frightened. "Mama?"

He could not answer. He put the receiver back onto its rest and moved painfully back into the bedroom and sat on the side of the bed and looked down at her.

"Don't do this," he said again. "Don't."

He did not hear them entering the house and the room. He saw his son-in-law, worker-strong, lifting her and placing her on the bed beside him, and he knew the daughters — there were two living close and the one he called had called the other — were talking frantically, saying words to him that he did not understand or did not care to hear. And then there were men with a stretcher, and he could feel the muscled arm of another son-in-law helping him to his walker, and he was in the hospital where the antiseptic smell of medicines flowed into his senses and he was aware of other daughters, hastily called, and one of his sons.

His son led him to a chair near the bed and he sat, holding his son's hand, and watched as his daughters approached her, leaned to her, whispered in small-child voices, "Mama? Mama?" And his son, the youngest of their children, a large, strong man, cried in a large, strong voice, like a prayer flung from his throat, "Old woman, I love you." He could feel his son's hand tighten in his hand. His son was sobbing.

He saw her push her head into the pillow and she opened her eyes and her lips parted, but she did not speak. Her eyes drifted across the faces of her children, then turned to him, held on him, closed. She swallowed once.

"Daddy?"

He opened his eyes and looked up. It was his oldest living son, who had driven the greatest distance in the dark May evening, across the mountains from Tennessee.

"It's late, Daddy. I think you'd better go to bed," his son said. The voice of his son was baritone and gentle, an orator's voice.

"What time is it?" he asked.

"A little after one," his son answered.

"That late?"

"Yes."

He had slept remembering her dying, and he did not know it. He thought again: It does not take long to die.

"The others are here," his son said.

He turned his head toward the kitchen door. His other children were cuddled, touching one another, staring at him. His children seemed very old to him.

"We're all about to get settled in for the night," his son told him. "Some of us will be here with you. We just wanted to say good night."

He nodded and pulled himself forward in the chair and caught his walker with his hands. His son helped lift him. He could feel a burning in his bad leg.

"Do you hurt?" his son asked.

"A little."

"You want something, Daddy?" asked one of the daughters.

"I gave him some aspirin," another daughter answered.

"I'll be all right when I get to bed," he said.

"We'll get the doctor to give you something stronger tomorrow," his oldest daughter said forcefully. "He'll do that."

He stood leaning against his walker. He could hear the static of the swamp bugs, but not the whippoorwill. There was a pause, an uncomfortable lapse of time, an off-beat hesitation. His oldest living son embraced him. "We love you," his son whispered. And they all came to him, bending across his walker, each embracing him, each mumbling to him, each stepping away, back into the cuddling of the group.

He looked at them. He could feel his head nodding. He said, almost numbly, "We'll miss her."

One of the daughters cried very suddenly, "Mama! Mama!"

TWO

There were many flowers at her funeral and many people, and he believed she would have approved of the service, though, for him, the preaching in the eulogy was a message of panic rather than promise — "Everybody's going to die. Get ready for God now, while there's time. O sinner, nobody knows the time. Nobody knows but Jesus. Amen. Amen. Amen." — and he tired of the singing trio with its off-key whine conjuring up images of angels and an old rugged cross and a gathering at the river.

He had always missed her intensely when crossing rivers, going away to work in other places. The rivers had been a ground-rip in the space that separated them. Yes, we shall gather at the river. Gather. But why? Gather to wait? Gather to stare across? Gather to hear the waters rushing?

He wanted to touch her face.

"Remember this day," the Preacher said to him and to his sons and daughters and grandsons and granddaughters. "Remember the passing of this loved one."

On the night of her death, he had taken from his desk the journal that he kept daily and he had written:

Today my wife died. We were married 57 good years.

It was the simplest entry he had ever recorded.

He would not forget the day. The Preacher would. But he would not.

He was led from the sanctuary of the funeral home where the service had been performed (her desire) to the car of his oldest living son and was driven to the gravesite where his oldest son — not living, but dead — had long been buried, and there he listened to a final, toneless litany. The Preacher paused before him, bowed just so at his gravesite chair, offered a handgrip and supplicant mutterings, and then moved to his sons and daughters, repeating himself like a parrot.

"Let's go home, Daddy," one of his sons said.

"In a minute," he replied.

The coffin was before him, balanced on strong nylon straps like a prop in an aerial act. A blanket of roses covered the chest of the coffin. He looked at the dug grave and, beside it, the grave of his oldest son — smooth mound, brilliantly white, glittering with mica dust — and he wanted to be alone. He could feel a hand on his shoulder.

"All right," he said softly. "All right." He stood at his walker. He could sense eyes staring at him. "Goodbye," he said to the coffin. He turned on his walker and moved away.

It was a day of sun — warm, bright, a soft wind from the west. The earth was green. The sun felt good on his face and hands.

In the afternoon, he took the druggist's pill and went into his bedroom and slept and dreamed of Neelie, the Negro woman who had worked with his wife. In his dream, Neelie was sitting beside his wife's coffin, talking to it. "I'll put up the beans. Don't you worry none. And cook up the biscuits, just like you been doing. Don't you worry none about it, none at all. I'll be around, taking care." And from the coffin, in a voice from the roses, his wife answered, "Put his water glass on the table, Neelie. Put ice in it. He likes it that way. And salt and pepper. He'll be asking for his salt and pepper." And Neelie said, "Oh, yes, I will. All them things. Don't you go worrying none. You just go on over and don't be worrying none about it. Neelie's here."

When he awoke he could hear voices through the walls of the bedroom. The house is still crowded, he thought. The church committee of women, there to clean and cook and grieve, would still be placing food on the tables and there would still be buffet lines of visitors picking at the sorrow feast. He wondered if Neelie was there, with them, telling them what needed to be done. Neelie had rushed into the house when she learned of his wife's death, had stormed loudly inside, shoving past children and grandchildren, and had embraced him with a squealing cry of torment. "Don't you worry none," she had said in a wail. "Neelie's here. Neelie's here."

He could hear the smaller grandchildren outside, playing.

"Patty's it."

"No, she's not. Patty's already been it. Greg's it."

At the funeral home, one of his daughters had said, "This is only the second time we've all been together, in the same room. The first time was the anniversary. You remember, Daddy? The fiftieth anniversary for you and Mama?" And the funeral director had asked — for the obituary notice — how many grandchildren there were in the family. No one knew, and so the director had taken his pen and written down the name of each child and that child's husband or wife in parentheses, oldest to youngest, and the number of children each couple had. The children were Alma (Hoyt), Lois (Tabor), Sam, Jr. (Melinda), Kate (Noah), Carrie (Holman), Paul (Brenda) and James (Saralyn). When the director added the number of grandchildren, the number had been twenty-eight.

"You'd think somebody would know how many grandchildren there are," Sam, Jr. had said.

"Mama did," Lois had answered. "She was the only one."

He did not leave his bed until late, after the visitors and the church committee of women left. He ate a bowl of soup (made by Neelie; she had remained) and listened to his daughters speak of house-cleaning. He knew he could not object, though the house-cleaning was only part of it. They would want to watch over him now, hovering. For a time, at least. They would want to study him, like an uncertain experiment. They would want to know if he could care for himself. If he could not, they would want to say what should be done for him.

"We won't be in the way, Daddy. We just want to get things straightened up."

"There'll be a lot of thank-you notes to write. We'll take care of that."

"Anytime you get tired of us, you can just tell us to leave."

"Daddy, you think you'll be all right here by yourself?"

In his journal, late at night, he wrote:

This is the saddest day I have lived in my 81 years. My wife of 57 years was buried today beside our son, who died in 1941 as a result of a truck accident when he was hitchhiking to take a job. She has longed for him all these years and now she is with him. I know they are embraced in happiness. Today ended for me a lifetime of joy and I am grateful to the Almighty for giving me the wife I wanted and the children we both wanted. Times were not always easy and I wished often that I could provide more than I was able to, but I can say that we had things that money could not buy. I will miss seeing her face and hearing her voice and knowing she was always there close to me. She has crossed a river from me that I must wait to cross before I see her again. When I see a river, I will think of her. All of our children have been here. They are very kind.

Again he took the druggist's pill and again he dreamed of her. She was in the kitchen, at the cabinet counter, kneading dough. Two of their daughters were with her in the kitchen, working.

"He'll be marrying again when I go. You'll see. He'll be marrying again. Find him some woman to come in here and do the cooking, some woman to take care of him. You'll see."

"Mama, don't say that."

"You don't know him. I do. You'll see. Somebody else'll be living here, making him biscuits with my biscuit cutter, three times a day."

"Is that right, Daddy?"

"That's right. But she won't have to cook a lick. Gonna find me a woman from one of them leg shows out in Atlanta."

"Daddy!"

"He will, too. Find some old woman, hiking her skirts. Maybe Sybil Hillard. She's had her eye on him twenty, thirty years. Used to come around at the canning plant when your daddy was running it. Didn't know beans about canning. But he'd do it for her. Didn't think I noticed, but I did."

"Mama, that's just being silly. Sybil Hillard's one of the

nicest women around here. She's got a husband. They must have been married forty-five years."

"You don't know her like I do. I remember her at the canning plant."

"Daddy, is that so?"

"I don't remember Sybil Hillard ever being at the canning plant."

"See, Mama."

"But she's a fine-looking woman, all right."

"Daddy, stop it!"

"Let him go on about her. I don't care. You wait and see. You just wait and see. There'll be somebody here making biscuits."

He awoke with the dream still clear in his mind. He smiled easily. The dream pleased him.

THREE

His daughters returned the following day to clean the house, and Neelie was there, also — not because she had been asked, but because she insisted and none of his daughters knew how to object.

"How can you tell her she's not needed?" they said among themselves. "She thinks she's got the right to be here. Ask her. She'll tell you. She'll tell you she's been around longer than any of us, helping out when Mama needed her."

And: "She'll be telling us what to do, that's for sure."

And: "I guess she will. She always has."

And: "Seems to make Daddy feel better, having her here."

And: "Maybe she thinks we'll be taking things out of here without her permission."

He did not stay in the house with his daughters and Neelie. He got into his truck and drove it to the edge of the field and got out of the truck and began to work in the small nursery plot of pecan trees, pulling away weeds, laboriously pushing himself from tree to tree with his walker. He thought of himself as an ancient turtle, dragging in inches across the crust of topsoil, legs clawing and legs pushing, stopping, resting, moving, resting again. But it did not matter. He was at peace in the nursery plot. Once he had had acres of trees growing out for the selling, but now there were only a few rows. She had not wanted him to plant them, but he had. "No need of it," she had said. "You can't get about on that walker as it is. Can't take care of them. No need of it." And he had argued, "I'll go easy with it. Just put out a few, just enough to have some on hand if people want them." But he had known, even when he planted the seeds, that the trees were for him, not for people who may want them. He liked the growing of them, liked the surgery of budding and the smell of the wood and the pruning of limbs. "They'll be the last," he had promised, and she had scowled at his stubbornness. She had said, "You get to hurting, and see if I run off to get you some medicine. No sense in it. You got trees all over this county. No need to be growing any more."

He moved along the row of trees, setting the walker, leaning his weight onto it, feeling the walker sink into the topsoil, slowly, slowly moving, pulling at the dead weeds of winter and the new, tender weeds of spring, shaking the soil from roots of the new weeds, throwing the weeds, roots up, into the middle of the row to wither in the sun.

He looked back down the row, at the peculiar tracks he had made — the single, hard footprint, the four punch-holes of the walker. He looked at the slender stalks of the trees, at the pulled grass in the row's middle. He had not moved more than fifty feet in two hours. Old turtle, he thought. Going nowhere slow. The sun gathered like a pillow in his hat and across the bridge of his shoulders.

At lunch he would take the druggist's medicine and sleep, but he did not want to be in the house now, not with his daughters and Neelie rummaging like thieves through cabinets and closets and drawers, filling boxes to be carried away. They would take away much of her in the trunks of their cars, leaving just enough for her to be vaguely present. A jewelry box. A robe in a closet. A hat for Sundays. Slippers. A shoe carton of letters. Enough for him to see her in rooms, like fragments of telltale clues in a shallow mystery. But there was no mystery. She had died, and his daughters — their daughters — and Neelie were removing her, room by room. They would work quickly, he thought, agreeing among themselves that it was best for him not to see what they were doing. And he would not question them. It was their ritual — a rite of daughters. And of Neelie. Neelie deserved to be there. Neelie knew the house better than any of them.

He stood upright and stretched the muscles of his back and then took his handkerchief and rubbed the perspiration from his forehead and eyes and from the band of his hat. Then he fanned his face with the hat.

There would be only one place his daughters and Neelie would not clean, he reasoned: his desk. The desk was private. None of them had ever opened his desk or asked about its contents. "Don't bother the desk," she had warned their children. "That's your daddy's. Leave it alone." And their children had obeyed and had passed the warning to their children and they, too, had obeyed.

The desk contained his records and letters and journals. The records and letters and journals contained his history, and hers and the history of their children, written in the shorthand of days and seasons and years. Children born. Dates, names, weights. Measles and chicken pox and mumps and broken bones. Date occurred, date healed. Year by year. The planting of crops, with free-hand drawings of contour maps. Year by year. Date planted, date harvested, yields, prices, net-from-gross sums. Cow names, cow breedings, calves dropped, calf names. Tree seeds planted, trees budded, trees sold. Droughts. Freezes. Gain, loss. Gain, loss. Year by year. His letters and records and journals were like orderly albums of photographs — words in odd, staring poses. But no one had ever opened his desk or asked about its contents.

He could hear the sharp clap of a door closing, and he twisted his weight on the walker, propping on his good leg, and looked toward the house. Neelie was crossing the yard in a long stride, her arms swinging in exaggeration like a triumphant swim stroke. She has them doing what she wants done, he thought. Exactly. Neelie was in command. It was in her walk, in the erect carriage of her slender, tall body, in the polished, hard blackness of her face. Neelie was in charge of the house-cleaning and his daughters were helpless to stop her.

Neelie crossed the road and followed the path under the orchard of pecan trees near the field. She stopped at the edge of the pecan rows. Neelie had worked most of her life in the fields. On her sixtieth birthday she had vowed never again to walk into one.

"Not even if Jesus told me to," she had said defiantly.

"You come on to the house and eat you something," she called in her high, shrill voice. He waved his hand and nodded.

"Don't you go pulling up no more of them weeds," Neelie ordered. "Too hot out here for old folks like me and you. You get yourself back inside before you go falling out. Lord, Jesus, Neelie can't lift you up, you go falling out."

He waved again and turned carefully on the walker and began to move back down the row, over the pulled, withering grass. Neelie stood watching him, arms crossed. She was talking rapidly (scolding him, he guessed), but he could not hear what she said. He knew it would be useless to argue with Neelie. She would badger him with her voice until he surrendered. And it was hot. And he was tired. Neelie watched him until he reached the end of the row and his truck. "You need some help?" she asked in a loud voice.

"No," he said.

"Lord, Jesus, I swear you gon' kill yourself in that old truck," she complained. She shook her head in disgust and began striding back to the house.

He lifted the walker and put it into the bed of the truck and, holding to the door handle, pulled himself up into the cab. No one trusted his truck, or him in it. He did not have a driver's license, but he did not care. The truck was a grand possession — old, paint bleached to the metal and the metal stained with rust. Its motor banged, parts hammering against parts. Its gears were loose.

"What gear you got it in, Daddy?" his sons and daughters would ask.

"I don't know. One that moves," he always answered.

The truck jerked like an animal shuddering under its skin. But it was his truck. His. He could no longer walk over his land, and the truck carried him, two sluggish old things getting about. Let them snicker and shake their heads in pity. It was his truck, by God, and he loved it. And his grandchildren loved it. His grandchildren were always pestering him to take them for rides.

He did not inspect the house or ask his daughters about the boxes stacked on the sideporch. He went into the kitchen and sat at the table where Neelie and Lois and Carrie were sitting, polishing silverware. Alma and Kate were clearing cabinets, stacking the contents on the counter.

"Neelie made you some oyster soup," Neelie said to him proudly, knowing he liked the soup. "Carrie, get up and get your daddy a bowl of that soup," she directed.

Carrie moved from her chair and ladled the soup into a bowl and placed it before him.

"Get him some water while you up, honey," Neelie added. "You know your daddy likes his water on the table."

Carrie did as she was told. He ate the soup slowly — it was thick and hot, the way he liked it — and listened as Neelie jabbered in her weapon-voice, telling loud, exaggerated stories of his sons and daughters as children. Stories of temper fits and tears and runaways and ghosts and awe. His daughters listened and nodded politely, irritated smiles fixed on their faces, and he knew they were annoyed because Neelie was not properly solemn for such a properly solemn occasion.

"Jesus, Lord, Carrie here was the worst of them all. Always coming to me, saying, 'Neelie, Mama done whipped me and I ain't done nothing.' And she'd throw her little fit and say she was gon' run away from home."

"I didn't do that, Neelie."

"Jesus, Lord, honey, yes you did. One time, you made Neelie pack you some runaway brown-sugar biscuits, and you went off down in the pasture and ate every last one of them and come back home at sundown, sick to your stomach."

"I don't remember that, Neelie."

"Honey, you wadn't but a little bitty thing. Little bitty things don't remember nothing. You was a mess, honey. Not like Paul. He was the sweetest thing you ever saw when he was little. Always helping Neelie. Only thing Paul ever done was get left behind in town one day, when your mama took everybody in with her. Jesus, Lord, they was so many babies she done forgot about having Paul, and she come all the way back home. And when they go back to find him, they wadn't the first sign of that baby. Not one. He wadn't but four or five. Your poor mama most went out of her mind, worrying about him, saying he was done snatched up by somebody and took off. Bless his soul, he done went dead to sleep in the dime store, up under some boxes. They found him around about nightfall. Jesus, Lord, he was a good baby. Ain't no wonder to Neelie he come out a preacher."

He remembered the day. She had cried in great horror that their son, their good son, would be lost. One son had already been lost and the pain of his death had never left her.

The stories rained from Neelie. Her voice became a caw, like a bird's fuss. She sat at the end of the table, near the windows, her thin, brittle body rocking rhythmically against the chairback, her long hands and fingers fluttering, skimming across her forearms and then her face — forearms and face, forearms and face. The doctors had told Neelie that she had a disease of the nervous system — she could not pronounce it and could not explain it — and they had given her a prescription that she carried always in her purse like a prize. Yet, when she became excited, or agitated, the medicine did not work and she could not stop her hands from moving or trembling, but she had trained her hands to the control of touching forearms and face, like a repeated signal of distress. Now, with the daughters of her dead friend, Neelie was excited. She was again among them, again listened to, again important.

"Jesus, Lord, it's a wonder we raised these children, ain't it, Mr. Sam?"

"I guess so," he said. He liked Neelie. Neelie had tended all but the oldest of their children, Alma and Thomas, and she had treated them with off-balance moods of discipline ("Neelie's gon' cut a switch, you don't straighten up.") and favoritism ("Honey, you know Neelie loves you more'n anybody on God's green earth."), and in the uncertainty of those quick moods, she had always been triumphant. Her lamentation had always been tragic and noisy: "Poor old Neelie, honey. Poor old Neelie. Ain't got nothing, don't know nothing. These babies don't even like to be around poor old Neelie." And the babies — his babies — would hold tightly onto Neelie, begging to do something to keep her from being poor. It was a soliloquy that had worked when the children were very small, and it worked when they became adults. Once a visitor had asked Kate if Neelie belonged to the family, saying the word "belonged" with the acid of cynicism, and Kate had answered, innocently, "No. We belong to Neelie."

"You get anything to eat, Neelie?" he asked.

"Had me some oatmeal this morning, Mr. Sam," Neelie said sadly. "Can't keep much more'n oatmeal on my stomach. Arlie's coming by in a minute to pick me up. Neelie's got to go feed that bunch of his."

"How is Arlie?" Carrie asked.

"He's fine, honey. Arlie's a good boy. Runs around with a

bad crowd sometimes, that sorry bunch of white boys over on the Goldmine ridge. Them boys ought to be put under the jail, they so sorry. Sorriest bunch I ever saw, white or colored. Always stealing or running moonshine liquor. But Arlie's all right when he ain't with them. It's that bunch of his that keeps me going. Jesus, Lord, them grandbabies don't know poor old Neelie can't go like she used to. Way they eat, they got worms. Never saw such. Eat all the time. All Neelie does, honey, is stand over the stove."

"Why don't you take some of these sandwiches we made for lunch?" Alma said. "There's a lot more than we're going to eat."

Because Alma was the oldest of the children and because Neelie had not tended to her as a child, Alma was the only one who made Neelie feel uncertain.

"Honey, I couldn't do that. Can't take food out of the mouth of my babies here to put it in the mouth of babies somewheres else."

"It's all right," Alma said evenly.

"Neelie, you know you wouldn't be taking food away from us," Carrie argued. "You know we got more than we need. We'll put some of these sandwiches in a bag for you."

"Well, honey, do what you want to do," Neelie said, her voice softening to exhaustion. "I ain't gon' argue none with my babies. It'd keep Neelie from standing over a stove. Guess I done pushed myself a little too much this morning, being here with my babies. Jesus, Lord, I love you children. And I loved your mama. She was the best person I ever met, white or colored."

Neelie was still talking when Arlie arrived. She was still talking, still giving orders, when Carrie followed her through the back door and to the car. She was still talking, thrusting her head out of the car window, when Arlie drove away.

In the kitchen, his daughters stood numbly, staring at one another. A piercing ring, the echo of Neelie's voice, seemed suspended in the silence of the room. "What's the matter?" he asked teasingly. "Neelie wouldn't let you talk?"

"I've got a headache, Daddy."

"She didn't stop talking the whole morning, not a single minute."

"I swear, she's been bossing us from day one and she's never let up."

"Well, she's been around long enough to belong, I guess."

"You can't forget how much of a help she was to Mama when there were so many of us at home."

"That's true. And she did love Mama. And Mama loved her."

"Did anybody pay her?" he asked.

"No," answered Alma. "I offered, Daddy, but she said she didn't want anything. Said she just wanted to be here to help out. Said it was little enough for what Mama had done for her." Alma sat in the chair beside him. "Daddy," she said, "you'll have to be careful about Neelie wanting to come over here to help out. She'll want to do that, especially for a while."

"It's all right," he said. "She won't be able to do much, but I won't need much done."

"We just want you to know that it won't be necessary," Alma said gently. "We'll be here. All of us. I know some of us live away, but Kate and Carrie are right here, and the rest of us can make arrangements. We can help out, too."

He nodded. He stared at the empty soup bowl and played with the handle of the spoon. He knew his daughters did not think he could live alone. His daughters did not trust his age. His daughters were afraid for him.

"Did you take your medicine?" Carrie asked.

"I will in a minute," he said. He could sense his daughters moving close to him, hovering. The tired, parchment face of his dying grandfather flashed in his mind.

"You're not going back out in this heat, are you?" asked Alma.

"Maybe later, when it cools off."

"Daddy, you're going to worry us to death if you keep going out in those fields by yourself," Kate said fretfully. "You're just going to have to promise us you'll stop it."

He looked at his daughter. She lived in the house near his plot of pecan trees. When he worked among the trees he could see her standing at her living room window, watching him. He said, "Well, I guess you're just going to have to worry. I know what I can do and what I can't. If you want to worry about it, that's up to you."

His daughters retreated from him in silence.

He could not hear them from his bed. He knew they were being deliberately quiet, waiting for the druggist's medicine to seize him and lull him into sleep. The house was strangely quiet, quieter than he had ever realized. The house had always whispered to him — wall and floor and ceiling voices — but now it was silent, and he thought: So this is it. This is what it will be when they leave. Quiet. Quiet, deep as velvet. Quiet beyond silence. The house had always known noise — giddy, screaming, angry, crowded noise. And now he was the only leftover of that noise. He rubbed the ache in his leg. He could feel the medicine oozing through him, flushing his skin with heat. He rolled to his elbow on the bed and raised his head and looked out of the bedroom window. At the edge of the yard, against the wheat-brown of broom sedge in the unplanted field, he saw a flash of white, low against the ground. He pulled the pillow against his head and closed his eyes. The medicine reached the stem of his neck, flowed like a vapor into his brain, coated against his forehead, and he slept.

For another week, there was always someone with him — Lois and Tabor from South Carolina, Paul and Brenda for a weekend, Sam, Jr. and Melinda for three days mid-week, the nearby Kate and Carrie with their daily coming and going, bringing him food from their tables. The arrivals and leavings of his children were deliberately and smoothly timed, like runners in a relay, and their transparent, covert planning amused him.

"Oh, I didn't know you were here."

"Haven't been long. I was just leaving."

"Can't you stay a few minutes?"

"Wish I could, but I've got to go. Daddy's looking good, don't you think? You are, Daddy. You look good."

"Yes, he is. Real good. See you soon?"

"Sure. I'll be dropping back by."

He said nothing to them of their frantic scheduling. He pretended that he was not aware, but at night he would make notes in his journal:

Carrie arrived at 8:30 with breakfast. She left at 10:30
when Lois arrived. Lois stayed through lunch. She left at
3:00 when Kate arrived. Maybe they think old people are
also dumb.

They were watching him carefully, not wanting him to know
but betraying themselves with their faces and with their poor
acting of poor scenes, and he knew they were talking constantly
about him in telephone calls to one another, saying, "What do you
think? How's he doing? Is he bearing up? What should we do?
What?"

And then the time between the leavings and arrivals began
to increase — at first, a few hours, and then a day, and then two
days. And he realized his children had made their decision: they
would inch cautiously away from him, giving him time and space.
It was their weaning of him, their reluctant admission that he
wished to be alone.

On a Sunday night, he wrote in his journal:

My son James and his wife Saralyn came to visit today and
Saralyn cooked a good lunch, as she always does. Kate and
Noah stopped by after church and ate with us. Brenda
called to say Paul had a funeral service to conduct. I
have good daughters-in-law in Brenda and Saralyn and
Melinda. Alma and Hoyt arrived about three o'clock and
we had leftovers for supper. Hoyt fixed the radiator in my
truck, where the hose had been leaking for a few days.
Hoyt is the only person who knows my truck better than
I do. I am grateful to my children for wanting to take care
of me, though I can manage all right for myself. Before I
married their mother, I "batched" for several years and
avoided poisoning myself and kept a clean enough room.
I know my children are concerned about me, but I am all
right and I am glad they are letting me have a few days
to myself now and then. Their mother taught them to care
and I see her hand in all of this. I guess I should think
of it as her staying around to watch over me. But they've
got their own lives to live.

FOUR

He saw the dog through the window near his roll-top desk. It was morning, pre-dawn. He had awakened with a burning in his stomach and had mixed a glass of baking soda and water in the kitchen, and after he had taken it, he had gone back into the middle room to sit at his desk. On mornings when he awoke early he liked to sit and watch the sun rising from the fogcap that billowed nightly over the waters of the swamp. The sun would lift out of the spreading silk of the fogcap, and balance itself, impaled, in the tree tips of black gum and oak. Always there was a moment — a quick slip of time — when the sun broke free of the trees and bled from its yolk, spilling in red-orange rivers over the silk. It was, to him, the most awesome spectacle in the universe.

He had not switched on the lights of the house. He knew if his daughters who lived near him saw the lights, they would worry and call him or send their husbands to inquire about him, and the peace that he enjoyed would be interrupted.

The dog was on the steps of the back porch, licking the cement with its tongue. He knew there were grease spots on the cement steps, where it had dripped the day before from a cooking pan as he carried the pan, precariously balanced on the grip of his walker, to the pasture fence to be emptied. He'd left the splatterings to be washed away in the next rain.

Dog's starving, he thought. Belly thin, ribs showing in its ribcage, licking at grease spots. Scared, too, by the look in its eyes and the way its ears were down against its skull. Maybe run off on its own from some place where it had been tied and badly treated. Maybe thrown out of a car somewhere along the creek, left to die.

Watching the dog angered him. Dog like that ought to be put out of its misery, he thought. But maybe it was close enough to dying on its own. Odd-looking dog. Whitest dog he'd ever seen. Nose as long as a greyhound's, tight-muscled over the back legs. He remembered the flash of white from the broom sedge and wondered if what he had seen had been the dog. But that was days ago, and he'd not seen it again, though he had looked, out of curiosity. Not likely, he decided. A dog that hangs around, looking for food scraps, makes itself seen to play on pity. He could afford pity, was, in fact, quick with it, but he could not afford to have a stray taking up at his back porch. He'd quit feeding strays now that his daughters lived close by and were tender to the woeful begging of animals that showed up out of the night.

He tightened his hands on his walker and pushed-walked back into the kitchen and to the back door. He could still see the dog through the kitchen window, sniffing, licking at the cement steps. He opened the door and pulled himself quickly onto the porch and, raising his walker in his hands, thrusting it before him, said, "Get! Get!" The dog leaped backward off the steps, falling on its side and rolling. "Get! Get!" he said again, striking his walker on the porch. The dog turned slowly, lowered its head and crept away, across the yard and road to the pasture's edge. There, in a nest of high grass, it dropped to its belly and stared back at the house.

"Hiding from me, huh?" he said softly. "Think I can't see you out there in that grass? Won't do you no good. I know you're there. Guess you been hiding out down there for days. Guess you think I didn't see you out there in the broom sedge."

He moved on his walker to the screened door of the porch and opened it and looked at the grease spots where the dog had licked. He could see strings of blood where the dog had cut its tongue on the cement. Must be sick, needing grease like that, he reasoned. Couldn't have survived without something to eat. Rabbits, maybe. But licking at grease spots like that must mean that it's sick. Rabies, maybe. Maybe in the early stages. He had once killed a dog with rabies, one snarling, slobbering at the mouth, but that had been a dog they'd hunted down in the swamps, one that had chased at people and animals.

He backed onto the porch and closed the screened door. Slow as he was on his walker, he couldn't have a dog rushing at him. He looked toward the pasture and saw the dog's face, a white dot in the grass. He knew the dog was watching him patiently. Best to get rid of it, he decided. Best thing to do. Run it off or kill it.

He remembered how she would become depressed and sullen when he killed the diseased, slow-dying animals that needed the kindness of euthanasia. He had finally stopped telling her about the killings. He had lied and said the animals had run off or he'd found them dead of their own causes and buried them. He did not know if she believed him, but she had pretended she did. There was nothing wrong with lies of mercy.

He moved back into the kitchen and set a pan of water on the stove to boil for his oatmeal and for his cup of instant coffee. He'd have Noah kill the dog, he determined. Noah was good with a gun, being a hunter. He'd do it himself, but the dog had the look of quickness, muscled across its back legs as it was, and he'd have to balance with the gun on his walker. Besides, his eyes were no longer clear enough for shooting. He'd do nothing but waste shells.

The thick, pewter gray of pre-dawn had thinned to shadowed light and he mixed the oatmeal, sugared and buttered it, and ate it at the table, watching the white dot of the hidden dog through the kitchen window. If she had been there, she would have fed it and then tried to shoo it away, as she'd fed beggars and sent them away during the Depression. Well, there was nothing wrong in that, he thought. Maybe it'll go off, if it has a full belly of food.

He did not finish the oatmeal (he ate sparingly now, even when his daughters filled his table with bowls of soft food and pushed it before him with worried urging), and he took the bowl and crumbled a day-old biscuit into it and spooned bacon grease from a cup over the biscuit and oatmeal and blended it. He then took the bowl to the steps of the back porch and left it and went back inside the house and sat in his chair beside his desk. Sitting, he could not see through the window over his desk, but he thought he heard the dog pushing the bowl across the cement, and later, when he checked, the bowl was empty. We'll see now, he thought. Maybe it'd go on and take up somewhere else, with some boy that would like to have a dog. If it didn't, he'd have Noah come out with his gun.

He saw the dog again at noon, as he crossed the yard to the mailbox. The dog was standing in front of the barn, looking at him. "Uh-huh," he said, nodding. "Uh-huh. Got brave, did you? Got you some food, and you think you're here to stay. Shouldn't've done it. Shouldn't've fed you." If the dog was not gone by nightfall, he'd call Noah. No use letting it hang around.

In the afternoon, Kate arrived to sweep the floors and change his bedsheets and he told her that he wanted Noah to come out with his gun later in the afternoon.

"Why, Daddy?" she asked.

"Got a dog hanging around out here," he said. "Looks about starved. Looks sick. Noah can put it out of its misery."

"What dog, Daddy? I haven't seen a dog."

"Well, it's here," he said. "Been around a few days, I'd guess. Saw it right after your mama's funeral."

"Funny that I wouldn't see it," Kate said. "Haven't heard any barking, either. You'd think Red or one of Carrie's dogs would bark if there was another dog around."

"Now, why would I make up something like that?" he asked irritably. "It was on the back steps this morning, licking up some grease I'd spilled. I chased it off, but I saw it down by the barn later on."

"Maybe it was just hungry," Kate said quietly. She sounded very much like her mother.

"Well, it'll just go on being hungry," he said. "I'm not going to go feeding it." The lie about not feeding the dog warmed him and he smiled.

"Funniest looking dog I ever saw," he said. "Looked like an albino. First dog your mama and I had looked just like it. Only other dog I ever saw as white."

"I'll tell Noah," Kate mumbled. "I'll have him come out." She added, "Don't know how I could miss seeing a dog like that."

Later, before sundown, Noah appeared with his hunting rifle in the crook of his arm and searched around the barns and in the pasture and fields, but he could not find the dog, and he left saying he would return the next day, but it was likely the dog had wandered off.

He said to Kate, "Your daddy must be seeing things. Can't be a stray dog hanging around out there. The rest of the dogs around here would be pitching a fit. We'd know it."

"Maybe he is," Kate admitted. "Maybe without Mama around to talk to, he's started imagining things. Things like that happen. I've read stories about it."

The next day and the day after and the day after, the dog appeared each morning on the steps of the back porch to eat from his leftover breakfast, and during the day, when he was outside with his walker, he would see the dog around the barns or in the fields, and he would call Kate and demand that she come out and see for herself.

But the dog would not show itself when Kate arrived, and she began to call her brothers and sisters and tell them that their father was hallucinating.

"Maybe the dog's hiding," her sisters and brothers suggested.

"It's not there," Kate said defiantly. "I've looked all over. Noah went by this morning on his way to work to see if it was at the porch, like Daddy says it always is, but it wasn't there."

"Maybe you're right," her brothers and sisters said sadly.

On the fourth day, after first seeing the dog licking grease spots, and seeing it every day following, he took his own gun and loaded it and leaned it against the jamb of the door leading to the back porch and waited for the dog to come to the baited bowl. But the dog did not appear. He remembered that he had heard rifle shots in the woods the day before. Maybe somebody had seen the dog and shot it. Maybe Noah. No, not Noah. Noah would have called him. It didn't matter. The dog was gone, and that was the end of it.

He sat for two hours at the kitchen table and stared out the window. That night, he wrote in his journal:

> White Dog, the dog that nobody can see but me, did not show up today and I believe it must be dead or decided to find a better table to beg from. Old biscuits and bacon grease must not taste

*too good. Whatever happened, it's better off. Being "slow of foot"
as I am, I would find it hard to care for a dog that appears to be
invisible to everybody but me. Cora and I had a dog that looked
just like White Dog when we lived in Tampa, right after we were
married. She also tried to hide from everybody but us. We found
her on the side of the road when she was just a pup and Cora had
me take her home with us. We called her Frosty, because she was
white like frost. I don't guess Cora ever loved another animal as
much as Frosty. She used to tell me that Frosty followed after her
when I was away at work. We kept Frosty until we moved back
to the farm and our first child, Alma, was born. A few days after
she arrived, Frosty disappeared. We could never find any trace
of her. I always thought somebody picked her up and took her too
far away to find her way back. It was another hot day. I don't
think it'll ever rain again. I remember it was this way in 1954,
when I was in the hospital with kidney stones and a slipped disc.
It didn't rain for weeks.*

He closed the journal and placed it back in the desk drawer
and sipped from his glass of homemade grape wine — sweet,
barely fermented. Tampa, he thought. She had been so young
then. And in awe of every new thing she could see and touch. The
orange orchards. The sea. Shrimp. Lobster. Crab. The rented
house on a paved street — their first house.

"It's not very large."

"It's what I want. Exactly what I want."

"We won't be here long. Just until the job's over."

"Maybe you can find another job, and we can stay."

"I don't know. Hard to get jobs."

And they had found the dog on the road, and she had taken
the dog up into her arms and cuddled it and wept because the dog
was hungry.

"I want to keep her."

"I don't know. Maybe she belongs to somebody around
here."

"Not out here. There's no houses around."

"I don't know if they'll let us keep a dog at the house."

"We'll find out. It'll keep me company, with you gone all day."

"She's not big enough to be a watchdog."

"I don't need a watchdog. Just something to keep me company, to keep me from being so lonely."

FIVE

He did not put the bowl out for the dog the next morning, or the next, and he did not see the dog. He was convinced the dog had left or had died. Left, most likely. He studied the sky for a sign of buzzards circling in a whirlwind of wings over a dead animal, but he did not see any buzzards and he decided that his morning bowl of oatmeal and biscuits and grease had become uninteresting to the dog and it had left in search of a more benevolent giver.

The dog appeared again on a Sunday evening, at dusk. He saw it beside the barn, beneath the hedge of Ligustrum. He whistled softly, and the dog lifted its ears and tilted its head.

"Come on," he called. "Come on. I got a biscuit in the kitchen." He started toward the dog on his walker, and the dog retreated, crawling backward until it reached the corner of the barn, then turned and slipped away out of sight. He did not follow. "Go on," he said angrily. "Get out of here."

The following morning, he left the bowl on the steps and watched from the kitchen as the dog appeared from behind the wellhouse and took the food hungrily. "Thought you'd be back," he said to himself. "Where you been?" He laughed quietly. "Don't even know what kind of dog you are. Must be a bitch dog. Maybe you been off having a time."

It was the morning that Neelie returned, as she had promised over his protests. He was at the kitchen sink, washing his breakfast bowl and cup, and he saw Arlie's car on the road that circled the house. He moved as quickly as he could on his walker into his bedroom and to the window that looked out onto the front yard. He saw Neelie emerging from the car, swatting at her grandchildren who crowded the backseat. He could not understand her words, but he could hear her voice, crowing orders to Arlie and to the grandchildren, and then the car pulled away. He thought, God Almighty, she's here for the day.

She did not knock at the door; she entered, calling his name: "Mr. Sam, Mr. Sam. It's Neelie, come to help out. Where you at, Mr. Sam?"

"In here," he answered. The door to his bedroom opened and Neelie stood in the doorway.

"You ain't still in bed?" she asked.

"No. I been up."

Neelie cackled a laugh. "Look at Neelie, standing here before a man's bedroom. Lord, Jesus, Mr. Sam, I didn't even knock. What if you was naked as the day you was borned?"

"I guess I'd of been naked," he said matter-of-factly.

"God love us, Mr. Sam, we'd of both fell out laughing. Put me'n you together, we old as the world. Too old to be getting shamed." A laugh rolled from her.

"I guess," he said, hobbling toward her on his walker. "I didn't know you were coming today."

"Just woke up feeling like it," Neelie said, stepping out of his way. "Neelie's been feeling poorly, for sure. Had a touch of them summer chills, like one of your babies used to get — Junior, wadn't it? Wadn't he handsome as the day is long at the funeral? Neelie sure would like to hear him preach the gospel, Mr. Sam. Sure would like to hear Paul preach the gospel, too. Both fine preachers, I hear tell."

He passed Neelie and went into the kitchen, and she followed, telling him that she had taken some medicine that Arlie had gotten her at the drugstore and the chill had passed in the night. He sat in a chair at the table, and Neelie sat opposite him.

"Old folks ought to stay in bed more'n young folks," she said profoundly. "That's when the fevers pass — in bed. Every time I get to feeling poorly now, I take to the bed, don't matter what them grandbabies want or what Arlie says needs doing. I take to bed and tell them to shut their traps and give old Neelie her rest."

"It helps," he said in resignation.

"Young folks don't know nothing. Jesus, Lord, I swear they

don't know nothing, Mr. Sam. They spoiled. You had you some breakfast?"

"Earlier," he told her. "Had some oatmeal."

"You got to eat, Mr. Sam. You got to, now. You got you any biscuits?"

"Had some left that Kate brought out."

"Neelie'll cook you some fresh ones. Ain't no need to go eating old biscuits. Them girls ain't been out here taking care of you, like they said they was?"

"They come out. Just about every day," he replied.

"They better. They don't, they have Neelie all over them, like a setting hen."

"They do a good job," he said. "Sometimes I wish they'd stay away more than they do."

"Ain't it the truth?" Neelie said emphatically. "Young folks worry you to death, you give them a chance. Every time you turn around, they all over the place. They don't know nothing about letting a person have some peace."

He nodded passively and stared out of the window. He knew it would be a hot day, too hot to work in his plot of pecan trees, but he knew he could not stay in the house and listen to Neelie. "How's Arlie doing?" he asked.

Neelie shook her head sadly. "He's gon' lose that job he's got over to the sawmill," he said. "Been hanging around that trash from the Goldmine ridge — them Morris boys. Folks saying them boys is been stealing, but ain't nobody know for sure. Said they was the ones that robbed that old couple over in Sardis a few days ago. Took all they cash money and some government checks they had. You got any cash money, Mr. Sam, you better hide it good. Keep you a shotgun by your bed, too."

"They wouldn't get much from me," he said. "I just keep enough for groceries."

"Well, you keep you a shotgun close by," Neelie said again. "Them boys don't care what you got or what you ain't got. They'll be thinking you got some insurance money after your wife die."

"I'll be careful," he said.

Neelie pulled from her chair, exaggerating pain. "Well, let Neelie get started working around here," she said. "Don't you worry about eating them old biscuits, Mr. Sam. Neelie'll cook you up some. Gon' throw all them old ones out."

"Just put them in a pan," he said. "I'll feed them to the dog."

"What dog you got?" Neelie asked. "I ain't seen no dogs."

"One took up the last few days. I put some food out every morning."

"Never seen so many stray dogs as what's out this year," Neelie said. "Don't trust them stray dogs. They soon as bite you as look at you. I swear they would."

"This one comes and goes."

"I'll put some biscuits aside," Neelie said. "You just go on in your chair and get to resting. Neelie's gon' clean up this kitchen." She looked at the table and cabinets and shook her head wearily. "Kitchen shows it when a man's in it. Neelie'll be cleaning all day in here."

He smiled. Kate and Carrie had been out the night before, cleaning the kitchen. Except for his dishes in the sink, the kitchen was in perfect order. "You see the girls, you ought to say something about it," he said. "When they come out, they don't like to work in the kitchen."

Neelie's eyes flared in disgust. "I will," she promised. "Them babies know better'n leave a kitchen looking like this."

He left the house and went to his barn to work, building a shelf for storage. He did not need the shelf, but he had been a carpenter before becoming a nurseryman (his father and grandfather had also been carpenters) and he liked building things. Constructing the shelf, even if he had to tear it down and build it again, was preferable to the assault of Neelie's voice and Neelie's commands.

In mid-morning he saw Kate's car stop in front of the house and Kate and Carrie, with two of Carrie's children, rushed into the house. He laughed easily. He knew they had learned of Neelie's presence — calling for him, he guessed — and Neelie had complained bitterly of the condition of the kitchen and had summoned both of them to help her and to receive her lecture for being negligent.

When he returned to the house at lunch, Neelie was sitting at the kitchen table watching as his daughters prepared his meal.

She was talking in a shout: "You babies got to make sure he got enough food around here. Jesus, Lord, can't have him eating oatmeal every time he gets hungry. And I couldn't find the first piece of fatback. He's used to having his peas and beans cooked with fatback. Your mama made sure that was the way it was done. Fatback gives it taste, babies. Don't for the life of me know how them folks up north eat peas and beans without fatback cooked in. But they do. Millie went up there, up to Detroit, and when she come back, she went on about how I was using too much fatback, said they didn't use none at all up north. Cooked up some beans like they do up in Detroit. Dogs wouldn't touch them beans. Next time they's a hog-killing, you babies got to put up some fatback for your daddy."

His daughters were not talking. They worked, tight-lipped, putting the food for his lunch before Neelie.

"What's all that food for?" he asked innocently.

"Neelie said you were hungry, almost starved," Kate said evenly.

"No, not particularly," he said. "What're you doing out here?"

His daughters stared at him incredulously.

"They said they wanted to help out poor old Neelie," Neelie answered sweetly. "I told them they wadn't no need. Told them Neelie could do it, but they come on anyhow. They sweet girls, Mr. Sam."

His daughters stared at each other incredulously.

He examined the kitchen and nodded appreciatively. "You got the place looking good, Neelie," he said.

"I been working at it, Mr. Sam. I sure have. But these babies been helping out some."

"Uh-huh," he mumbled. "They do all right when they get started."

He smiled at his daughters and sat at the table.

"Where's the salt, babies?" Neelie said. Then: "There it is. Right on the table. Been a snake it'd of bit me."

"You eat yet, Neelie?" he asked, ignoring his daughters.

"I had me a bite, Mr. Sam. Neelie don't need much. The fever took the hungry out of me." She pulled herself wearily from the chair. "You go on and eat," she said. "Believe I'll go set a spell out on the front porch. Maybe they's some air stirring out there. Get me a little rest before I start the washing."

"We did the washing, Neelie," Carrie said.

"Uh-huh. Well, honey, Neelie'll look over the house. See if we left anything." She hobbled away, through the kitchen, through the middle room and the living room, and to the front porch, her complaining voice trailing in her wake. His daughters did not move until they heard the living room door close.

"Daddy," Kate said, controlling her anger, "do you know what we've been through?"

He sipped from the glass of iced tea. "Better'n you think," he said.

"We just cleaned this kitchen last night."

He tasted the creamed potatoes. The butter was rich in them. "What I thought, too," he said.

"Well, I don't know about Carrie, but I can't just drop everything I'm doing everytime Neelie gets on her high horse," Kate snapped.

"Me, neither," Carrie said in controlled whisper. "But, we do it. We always do. Every time."

"You ought to tell her that," he advised. "Peas taste good," he added.

"Well, maybe I will. Maybe that's just exactly what I'll do," Kate said bravely. "Maybe it's time one of us showed some spunk around here."

"She's out there on the front porch, I'd guess," he said.

"You don't think I'll do it, do you?" Kate said to her father.

He liked the spirit that burned proudly in her eyes. Kate had a wonderful temper, the same temper her mother had had. "Up to you," he said, after a moment.

"I'll go with you, if you want me to," Carrie said timidly.

Kate sighed. She rubbed the clean counter top with a damp cloth. "That'd be a great help," she complained. "The first thing that'd happen would be Neelie putting on that look like we've just whipped her with a leather strap, and you'd start to cry and that'd be that."

"Well, put the blame on me," Carrie said defensively.

"Don't go getting upset," Kate said. "You know as well as I do what I mean. It's Neelie's way."

"Both of you are making a mountain out of a molehill," he said. "What's she done that's so bad?"

"Neelie makes out you're starving, like we don't care what happens to you," Carrie sniffed. There were tears in her voice.

"What I told her this morning," he said.

"Daddy!"

"Oh, Carrie, he didn't say that," Kate replied. "You know Neelie."

"Well, I don't like her thinking that. She'll tell everybody that we don't care what happens to our daddy. You know how she talks. She's always telling us what goes on that nobody's sup-posed to know about."

"She's not going to say anything about us," Kate said.

"She talks about everybody else that way," Carrie argued. "What makes you think she won't talk about us?"

"Well, nobody pays it any attention," Kate said. She sat at the table and took food for her plate from the serving bowls. "Daddy," she said, "what's this about the dog? I thought you said it'd left."

"Guess it didn't," he said. "Showed up again yesterday. Here this morning." He looked at Carrie. "You going to eat?"

"When I find the kids. They're outside playing." She left through the kitchen door and he could hear her calling them.

"Daddy, I don't know why none of us can't see that dog," Kate said cautiously.

"I don't either," he said firmly. "It's there."

"I'm not saying it's not, Daddy. I'm — "

"Yes, you are," he said. "I know what you think. You think I'm seeing things. Think I've got some old-age crazy disease and I'm seeing things. Well, I can't help that."

"Daddy, it's not that. Not that at all. You know how stray dogs are. They show up everywhere, go house to house. They may sneak around, but they don't hide."

"This one does."

"Why?"

"How do I know? Could be that somebody beat it. Could be it don't like being around people."

"Could be," Kate sighed. "You don't think it's a mad dog, do you? You want Noah to come out here in the morning, be here when it shows up?"

He shook his head. "If it was mad, it would've shown it by now. If it's that stubborn about staying around, might as well give it a chance to live. No need killing something that's making it on its own. If it was in misery, that'd be different."

"I thought you said it looked like it was about dead."

"Don't look that way now."

"All right, Daddy."

He knew she did not believe him.

SIX

He put it in his mind to awake early and he did, in the pre-dawn. He cooked his breakfast as usual in the darkened kitchen, adding a single pad of hot sausage to his oatmeal diet, and when he had eaten his fill, he mixed the scraps in a bowl and placed it on the porch step. Maybe the dog had wandered away for the last time, he reasoned, and had returned to stay; besides, he had no other need of the scraps.

He bathed in a tub of hot water, hot as he could bear, and dressed in his work clothes and then slipped outside as the morning began to bubble in the east. He picked his way across the lawn, through the paling light, to a row of rose bushes that he could see from the kitchen window. She had planted the roses in that spot, near the hedgerow, to watch them grow and flower as she worked at her kitchen sink. She had loved the roses and jonquils and tulips and glads. He cut as many as he could carry in the basket that he had taped to the handgrip of his walker, and then he went back into the house and had his morning coffee.

He left the house through the back door. The bowl of breakfast scraps on the porch step was still filled, and he shrugged nonchalantly and moved to his truck and put his walker into the truck bed, beside the hoe he used in his nursery plot. He pushed the basket of flowers across the seat and muscled himself inside the cab. He could see the houses of both his daughters who lived near him. The houses were still dark. Won't be in a minute, he thought. He laughed silently. He knew that when his truck was started, lights would pop on in the houses of his daughters, and they would be urging their husbands to get out of bed and see why the truck was running. He knew that Kate would be bellowing commands to Noah, and that Carrie would immediately tele-phone Kate and ask, in her worried voice, what was happening. He turned the key and pushed the starter pedal with his foot. The motor boomed, like an attack, and the truck shook violently. "Don't start giving me trouble now," he said aloud. He pushed in the clutch and pulled at the gearshift and released the clutch and the truck bolted forward. He saw the lights snap on in unison in the houses of his daughters. He pushed hard against the accelera-tor, and the truck jumped, throwing him against the back of the seat. "Great God," he exclaimed.

He was at the bottom of the hill, at the flat of the pecan orchard, and going up the next hill before he realized he could not see the road well. He pulled at the light switch, but nothing happened. "Got to get Hoyt to look at that," he said. He squinted his eyes and slowed the truck. He did not need lights. He'd walked or ridden over the road for fifty years. All he had to do was steer between the two gullies. The truck was barely moving and he wondered if he should shift gears, but he did not. No reason to chance stopping altogether, he decided. He looked out of the window and blinked in surprise. There was the dog, leaping gracefully in the field beside the road, a white blur, like a burning star falling and rising, falling and rising. The dog was chasing him. "So you're still around," he said softly. "Yeah, I see you. I see you." The truck vibrated violently in the steering wheel, and he could feel the tickling in his hands. It was a good feeling. Two old things getting about, being chased by a dog no one could see.

He drove the backroads to the cemetery, trying to watch for the road, to stay between the gullies, and for the dog, but the dog was soon lost from his view. Probably got tired of chasing, he thought. But it'll be there when I get back, slinking around somewhere, waiting for a refill of the bowl.

At the cemetery, in the silvering of dawn, he took the hoe and cut away at the weeds, balancing on his walker, until the plot was clean. Then, kneeling between the graves of his wife and his son, he smoothed the sand mounds with his hands and divided the gathering of roses and placed them in buried vases. I have never placed flowers on the grave of my son, he thought. Never. It was something she did. I stood back and let her do it.

The death of their son was a grief that she could not release, and she had obsessively tended the grave, pushing him away with her sobs and her bitterness. It was the one thing they had never been able to resolve: she blamed him for their son's death. "Drove him away from home when he was too young," she had said. "Too hard on him. Too hard."

He touched the mound of his son's grave. A wave of tears hit him like nausea, and he began to cry openly. He pushed his hand deep into the mound, reaching for the son he had driven away.

He did not know how long he had been at the cemetery or how long he had sat between the grave mounds of his wife and his son. The day was bright, the sun had untangled from the trees and was in its stretch across the day, and on the highway nearby, cars rushed into the town. He looked at the tombstone. His family name was chiseled in bold letters across the face of the stone: Peek. His name and his wife's name and his son's name were in smaller letters. Names, dates. The same as in his journals. He looked at his own name: Robert Samuel Peek. The date of birth: October 16, 1892. A blank space was left for the date of death. Soon enough, he thought. Soon enough.

He gathered the hoe and flower basket and, holding to his walker, moved carefully back to his truck. The dog was under a tree near the truck, watching him. He saw it as he opened the truck door. "Found me, did you?" he said. He closed the door quietly and stretched out his hand to the dog. "Come on, come on. You that determined, you might as well come out of hiding."

The dog whimpered and dropped its head, but it did not move.

"Come on," he urged. "I'm not going to hurt you. You earned your right. Chased me all the way, did you? Guess it was easy enough, just following the racket." He made a soft whistling sound through his lips. The dog edged forward, pawing at the ground with its front feet. "All right," he said. "It's up to you. My walker's already put up in the back of the truck, and I'm not getting it down. You want to come here, you can, but I'm not coming to you. You got four good legs, I got one. You got me outnumbered. You do the walking." He squatted on his good leg, balancing with his right hand on the handle of the truck door. "Come on now," he said to the dog. "You think I'm going to beg, you wrong. You got about a minute before this leg gives out."

The dog inched its front feet forward, lowering its belly to the ground. It raised its head and began to whimper and crawl forward, and then it stood and crept to him, just beyond his fingers. "That's better," he said quietly. "You got another inch to go, and you better not bite. You bite me, I'll take that hoe to your head."

The dog stretched its nose to his fingers, touched them, then stepped forward and slipped the jaw of its head into his palm. "Good girl, good girl," he said playfully. "That's what you are, a girl."

He ran his hand under the dog's stomach. "What you are," he said again. "Good girl."

At midnight, alone, sleepless, he wrote in his journal:
Today marks three weeks since my wife, Cora, died. She was 75 years old. On the day she died she had been at the rest home, sitting with "old" people. She always wanted to be a nurse and she believed she had become one, spending her time with people who needed company. Being alone myself now, I understand how much she must have meant to them. I worked in the cemetery this morning, before it got hot. I put roses on the graves of Cora and Thomas. It was the first time I had ever put flowers on my son's grave. Cora always liked to do that and I knew it. I missed both of them while I was there, I guess more than I have ever missed anything. If the Almighty is willing, I look forward to the time I will be with them again. I finally got to touch the white dog today. She followed me to the cemetery and got up enough nerve to come to me. I tried to get her in the cab of the truck to ride back, but she wouldn't. Shows she has some sense, I suppose. I still don't know why she won't show herself when other people are around, but I won't question her. Carrie and Holman brought out some Brunswick stew for supper that Holman had picked up in Athens. It was hot with seasoning, the way I like it. We've gone a week without any rain.

SEVEN

It was his habit that he read daily from the obituaries in the newspaper and listened at the noon hour for the radio broadcast of hospital reports. It was no longer a surprise to him to learn of the death of someone he had known more than seventy years. "They're all dying," he said to his sons and daughters. "Not many left, not the ones I grew up with, but I don't guess it matters. Haven't seen most of them in forty years or longer."

It did matter when he read of the death of Hattie Lewis.

"I guess you could say she was my first little girlfriend," he confessed to his youngest son, James, who was visiting for the weekend. "Her name was Hattie Carey, before she got married. Of course, it was nothing like it is today. We didn't do anything but look at one another. I gave her a comb one time. Then all the boys started in on me about having a girlfriend, and I don't guess I spoke to her after that."

"Sounds like love, Daddy," James said, teasingly. "Did Mama ever know about this?"

He laughed. His eyes moistened in merriment. "Lord, no, son. She'd have had a fit. How old was I, then? Twelve? Maybe thirteen. Long time before I met your mama."

"Sounds serious to me, Daddy."

He laughed again. He liked his youngest son. It was a gentle family joke that James was an accident of passion, a mid-life surprise. And there was truth in the teasing, but irony in the birth. Cora had dreamed it before the pregnancy. She had dreamed there would be another male child, a replacement for her buried son. From the day she was certain of the pregnancy, she had declared, "This is a boy."

Even as his laughter over being teased about Hattie Lewis quietened, he remembered the day James had returned from Asia, a week earlier than expected. He was working in the field near the Civil War cemetery, and a car stopped on the road and James got out and crossed the field to embrace him. They set up a plan to surprise Cora — James circling the house to come in the side door, while he confused her with gibberish.

In the house, he said to her, "If you could have anything you wanted, what would it be?"

"What do you mean?" she asked.

"What would it be? If you could have anything."

She looked at him with a puzzled expression and with suspicion. "I don't know. A new car. Why're you asking?"

"That's it? More'n anything else, you'd want a new car?"

"Well —"

"Think about it. Anything you wanted."

Her eyes brightened suddenly, dampening, and her lips trembled. "I'd want to see my baby," she said softly.

And at that moment — that precise moment — James walked through the side door, behind her, and said, "Hello, Mama."

A chill struck him, caught in the smile that still carried his laughter. He had never seen her as joyful, holding her youngest son.

"Yeah, Daddy, that sounds serious to me," James repeated.

He took a swallow from his homemade grape wine and realized that was another reason he enjoyed being with James. He could drink homemade grape wine with James and not feel uncomfortable. James was not a preacher. He was an investigator for the U.S. Department of Alcohol, Tobacco and Firearms.

"She wound up marrying Neal Lewis, who was just a plain fool," he said. "Always doing some fool thing." He nodded his head to agree with his memory. The smile deepened in his face. He said, "One time, son, we had to recite a stand-up poem in school and the teacher — old lady Milbury — got to Neal and said, 'Stand up and do us your poem, Neal.' And Neal stood up beside his desk — I can see him now, just thinking about it — and said, 'Pecker-wood, pecker-wood, pecking on the door. Pecked so hard, his pecker got sore.'" He laughed hard, remembering the scene, laughed until the tears oozed from his small eyes.

"Sounds like a character, Daddy," James said.

"One time old lady Milbury was trying to explain that we belonged to the animal kingdom," he said, "and Neal was giving her the devil about it, saying he didn't believe one word of it. Said a cow was an animal, but he was a human. She said, 'Neal, what's the difference between me and a cow?' And Neal said, 'Cow's got four tits, you ain't got but two.'" Again he laughed until the tears seeped from his eyes, and he dried them with the tips of his fingers. "Never did know what Hattie saw in him," he said.

"Daddy, why don't I take you over to the funeral home to pay your respects?" his son suggested.

"I'd like that," he said. "I think I'd like that. I need to get me a haircut while we're out, too. And pick up a few things at the grocery store."

There were six men on the porch of the funeral home. They were sitting in a semicircle of rocking chairs when he arrived with James and walked his slow aluminum-legged walk across the lawn and to the porch. The men were sitting quietly, with the look of people enduring a familiar ritual. James was surprised that his father knew them and they him, and that the presence of his father seemed to interest them. They met with feeble handshakes and cackles and immediate old stories that had lapses of reason in the telling, and James could sense that for one energetic outburst of pushing away years they were again young and vigorous.

"Awful bad about Hattie," he said. "I read about it yesterday."

"Mighty fine lady," one of the men said in sympathy. Then, in an afterthought: "Seems like I remember you being sweet on her, Sam."

"Well, now, by shot, that's right," another of the men said. "What was we? Ten, eleven years old?"

"Lord, God," he said easily. He turned to his son. "Here we are, seventy years later, and they still making up lies, son."

The men laughed warmly.

"How's Neal holding up?" he asked.

"Doing all right," one of the men said profoundly. "He's gon' miss her, that's for sure. That woman straightened Neal out, much as he could be, I reckon. Sure to God, she did."

"Don't guess he's as big a fool as he used to be," he said.

The men laughed again, knowingly. "He was that, all right," one of them said. "Always has been, in his way. Hattie couldn't wash that out of him. She just starched him a little bit."

"Don't guess I've seen him in fifteen or twenty years," he said. "Not since I was in the Farm Bureau. Used to see him then, at some meetings. He was always cutting the fool, but everybody liked Neal. We went to New York on a convention one time. Got himself lost in a department store. He here?"

The men became solemn. "Inside there. His two daughters and his grandkids was here a few minutes ago. They left."

"Think I'll go in and pay my respects," he said.

"Good to see you, Sam," one of the men said to him, and the others mumbled agreement.

"All of us old folks ought to get together once in a while," another said.

"We don't ever do it," another added, "not to somebody dies. Then we sit around out here in these rockers, waiting our turn."

One of the men laughed suddenly, coughed, fought for his breath. "Crowd gets smaller every year," he wheezed at last. "Some of these days, they ain't but one of us gon' be sitting here."

"Yeah, and he's gon' be too damned old to talk," another said. "Just gon' be sitting here, staring off, looking at nothing, drooling down on his shirt." He giggled and nodded his head rapidly. "Ain't gon' be me. I guarantee that."

"It'll come to all of us, sooner or later," he said philosophically. He nodded to the men and the men nodded in reply, and then he turned on his walker and went inside the funeral home, with James following.

James signed the guest registry for both of them and asked a watching young woman which room contained the remains of Hattie Lewis. "The first room there," she said in a funeral voice. She pointed with a gesture of her head.

The only person in the room with the body of Hattie Lewis was Neal Lewis. He was sitting near the head of the coffin in a folding chair, his body bent forward, his elbows propped on his knees. He seemed to be in prayer, but he looked up when he heard the scraping of the walker. "Sam?" he said after a moment. "Sam Peek?" He stood.

"It's me, Neal. This is my boy, James. He drove me over."

Neal stepped forward and took his hand and then the hand of James. "Good of you to come over, Sam," he said. "Real good of you."

"Sorry to hear about her passing, Neal," he said softly. "Read about it in the paper yesterday. Heard it on the radio, too."

"We been expecting it," Neal said. "Ain't easy, though." He paused. "I guess you know how that is. I heard tell about your wife passing on. What was it? A few weeks ago? Hattie's been sick, and I ain't good about time these days."

"Few weeks now," he said.

"What I thought," Neal said. "Come here and look at her, Sam. They got her looking real pretty. Puffed up her face some. She'd wasted away to almost nothing."

He moved to the coffin and looked inside at the still, peaceful face of Hattie Lewis. Her face had been shaped by the mortician into a serene pose, almost a smile, as though she had simply blinked in the middle of a pleasant thought and had died and the thought had frozen on her face. He could still see the girl, taking the comb from him.

"Looks real nice, Neal," he said. "Real nice."

"They fixed her up real pretty," Neal said proudly.

"She was a fine lady."

"Best they ever was, Sam. She put up with me. God knows, that took some doing. Uh-huh, uh-huh. Guess we don't credit them enough while they alive."

"Don't guess we do," he said.

"Won't be the same without her, I know that."

"What time's the funeral?" he asked.

"Tomorrow at two. Out in the Sardis cemetery. That's where we been going to church since that falling out in town. We got us a plot out there couple of years ago, right after she took sick."

"I'll do my best to be there, Neal," he said. "Sometimes there's company on Sunday."

"I'll understand, you don't make it. I'm just glad to see you here," Neal said. He looked into the coffin. "Hattie would've been, too. She was always talking about what a fine family you got, having them preacher boys." He turned to James. "This one of them preachers?"

"Not me," James said, smiling. "That'd be my older brothers."

"Well, son, we can't all of us go preaching," Neal said. "Won't be nobody to preach to, if we did. Some of us got to give them preachers things to preach about. Guess I've turned up my share of sermons. Ain't that right, Sam?" His voice was playful.

"Never saw you do nothing mean, Neal," he said.

"Well, never tried to do nothing mean. Just couldn't turn down a dare when it was staring me in the face," Neal said. He moved close to James and whispered, "Truth of the matter, it was your daddy who was always coming up with them dares."

"That right, Daddy?" James asked. "You're responsible for getting Mr. Lewis in trouble?" He could see his father blush.

"I don't remember making any dares," he said.

"You remember old lady Milbury?" Neal asked.

He nodded and cleared his throat softly. He always cleared his throat when uncomfortable or when he wanted to make a point worth remembering.

"Your daddy wrote me a poem one time," Neal said to James. "Dared me to say it in class. Old lady Milbury like to have fainted. You get him to tell you about it sometime."

James smiled. "I will."

"Well, we got to be going on, Neal," he said.

"Glad you came by, Sam," Neal said solemnly.

"You come over to see me."

"I'll do that, Sam. I sure will. I'd like the company."

He talked late into the night with his son, sitting comfortably in his padded rocker, sharing his grape wine. He talked of Neal Lewis, vowing Neal had lied about him writing the poem, and he talked of the men on the porch of the funeral home and of crimson clover festivals and celebrations on the Fourth of July. James listened in amazement, realizing that his father had seldom spoken of his youth, and he urged the stories from him.

It was past midnight when he began to tire, and he drained the last of the wine from his glass. "They tell you about the dog, son?" he asked.

"Yes sir."

"Your sisters think I'm making it all up."

"I guess."

"Well, I'm not," he said wearily. "Don't know why in the world that dog won't show itself when somebody's around, but she won't."

"Don't worry about it, Daddy."

"Strangest thing I ever saw," he said. "Just shows up out of nowhere. I was down in the pasture yesterday, trying to find where Noah's cows were getting out, and there she was, big as day. Just came trotting up. Put her paws up on the side of the truck door. I had a biscuit in my pocket and I gave it to her and she swallowed it whole."

"That right?"

He laughed easily. "Guess I'd think the same thing if I couldn't see her. Guess I'd think I was crazy, too."

"Nobody thinks you're crazy, Daddy."

"I know, son. Just old. That's what it is. And just being old is about the same thing as just being crazy."

"Better get on to bed, Daddy," James said. "It's late."

"I will in a minute. You go on. I'm just going to sit here a few minutes."

"Yes sir."

He took his journal from his desk drawer and opened it to the date and found the red-tipped pen and wrote:

> Spent the day with James and we both have been up too late. James took me to get a haircut ($1.50) and a few groceries from Pennywise ($13.83) and then we went to the funeral home to pay respects to Hattie Lewis, who died two days ago of cancer. She was a special childhood friend. Talked to Neal Lewis, her husband, another childhood friend who was a cut-up in class. Saw some other old friends there, too. It seems that somebody out of the old crowd dies every few weeks now. Soon we will all be gone and everything will be left to the young people. It has been a pleasant day. Not too hot. With James here, I have not seen White Dog, but I will keep leaving food out for her in hopes that she will show herself. I'm beginning to think I'm crazy myself.

EIGHT

A hard rain began in the night, lashing in sheets from an unexpected west wind, and though he had slept pleasantly from the exhaustion of the day before and from the wine and the late hour with his son, he awoke early and went into the kitchen and warmed day-old biscuits from Kate and cooked sausage and made a milk gravy and called James to breakfast.

"Bad day for Hattie's funeral," he said, watching the rain lap against the house. "Don't guess I'd better try to go over."

"Don't think you should," James said. "Anyway, I thought Lois and Tabor were coming down for lunch."

"She said they might. Don't know now. One of the kids was sick and the road's slick now."

In mid-morning, James left to return to his home in South Carolina, and Lois called to say she and Tabor would not visit for lunch. He did not mind. He had spent long hours with his son for two days, surprising himself with the ease of his storytelling, and he had refused his afternoon naps. It would be a good day to rest. There was nothing that lulled him to sleep as quickly, or as deeply, as the drumming of rain, not even the druggist's medicines.

He listened to a radio sermon from a Baptist preacher who raved about foreign infidels soiling America with their oil-slick greed, and he thought about his sons who were, at that moment, standing in pulpits instructing people in the way of the Almighty. He had never been a man for churches, though he believed in keeping the Sabbath and in treating people fairly, and he believed most of all in the inexplicable power of something far grander than man or earth. He thought to himself, I ought to start going to church again. Surely my sons are ashamed that I don't. Maybe I'll transfer my letter from the Baptist church in Madison — if it's still there. It had been almost sixty years since he'd joined the church to please Cora Elizabeth Wills.

The radio preacher asked for five dollars from each listener, or whatever each listener could afford. The money was needed, the preacher declared, to keep his ministry-of-the-air alive and vigorous. The preacher promised in return a brochure of special scriptures that would assuredly comfort anyone in their most desperate needs. He wrote the name of the preacher and the address of the radio station on the back of an envelope.

He took the Bible — a gift from Alma that he kept displayed to please her — and opened it at Genesis and began reading. He read two chapters, to the verse that proclaimed:

> And they were both naked, the man and his wife, and were
> not ashamed.

That's the way it ought to be, he thought. But that was before the snake.

He turned back to Chapter One and scanned to the eleventh verse and he read it again:

> And God said, Let the earth bring forth grass, the herb
> yielding seed, and the fruit tree yielding fruit after his kind,
> whose seed is in itself, upon the earth: and it was so.

The Bible was wrong about that. Not at all the way fruit trees behaved. You wanted to get a certain kind of fruit, you had to bud for it. You couldn't take a Golden Delicious apple and plant the seed and have the tree bearing Golden Delicious apples like the parent tree. You had to take budwood from the parent tree and cut the bud out and slip it into the bark of the scion and then you'd get a Golden Delicious apple. But the way the Bible had it in Genesis was close enough. Certainly an apple tree would not produce pecans. It was something he would have to talk to his preacher sons about; see if there was something omitted in the translation.

And there were other things he would discuss with his preacher sons.

Adam naming all the creatures. It'd take time for that if they lined up one by one. The earth was full of creatures. It made a nice enough story, but it wasn't practical. It was like believing that

Noah put two of every creature — a male and a female — on the Ark. Who could believe that? It would have taken a boat the size of Hart County, and even then it would've been crowded. And what about the food to feed all those creatures? It'd have to be stored somewhere. But it was a nice story. He'd liked it when he was a boy, listening to Sunday School teachers telling about how God was in the old days.

He skipped Chapter Three. He knew about the snake and the apple and how Eve goaded Adam into taking a bite from the apple and how they became ashamed because they were naked and how God got angry and drove them from the Garden of Eden. And he knew about Cain and Abel and how Cain killed Abel in Chapter Four. He glanced at the names of the children and grandchildren of Cain—Enoch, Irad, Mehujael, Methusael, Lamech. Unpronounceable names. And that was another thing: Where did Cain's wife come from, if Adam and Eve were the first people on earth? Did God make some more people, somewhere else, and they got left out of the Bible? It was possible. One thing about them: they lived long enough. Eight hundred years. Nine hundred years. Methuselah was in there. Methuselah lived nine hundred and sixty-nine years.

He fanned the pages to Chapter Nineteen and saw the words:

> And there came two angels to Sodom at even; and Lot sat in
> the gate of Sodom: and Lot seeing them rose up to meet them;
> and he bowed himself with his face toward the ground.

Sodom. Sodom and Gomorrah, he thought. He knew about that story. Good-time Sodom and Gomorrah. God got even with them, smiting everybody but Lot and his family, warning them not to look back on his terrible destruction. But Lot's wife could not resist the temptation and looked back, and God had turned her into a pillar of salt. He had had a professor at Madison A&M who claimed Lot's wife was the first salt-lick. He smiled at the thought and he began reading from the chapter. His eyes widened with surprise at the thirty-first and thirty-second verses:

> And the firstborn said unto the younger, Our father is old,
> and there is not a man in the earth to come in unto us after
> the manner of all the earth;
> Come, let us make our father drink wine, and we will lie with
> him, that we may preserve seed of our father.

He read on, to the end of the chapter and the story of Lot's daughters bearing his children, then he closed the Bible. He'd have to ask his sons about that, about Lot's daughters. If a person wanted to argue the point, it could be said that the Bible contained a dirty story, he thought. And maybe that was why people were always debating it. He'd have to think about that before reading further. Even though he'd never been a churchgoer, he had always believed there was an Almighty. He had to believe that. How could he understand the growing of plants if he didn't? He could bud the trees to grow the kind of fruit he wanted, but he could not make the leaves unfold from the tips of limbs and flutter in the wind like small green flags. That was not his doing.

The man who delivered the Sunday paper brought the paper into the house for him, and he made a mental note to write about it in his journal — *The paper carrier did a neighborly deed for me, knowing I must use a walker . . .* — and maybe he would write a letter to the newspaper to compliment the carrier. There was nothing of great interest in the paper. He did not know any of the people listed in the obituaries, though he thought he had heard of one man from Anderson, a King Welborn. Maybe King Welborn had bought trees from him in the past. He took his order pads for the last ten years and leafed through the carbon copies of sales slips, but he could not find King Welborn's name.

He did not think about White Dog until after his lunch (soup from a can). He mixed the breakfast scraps, covering them with the congealed milk gravy, and went onto the back porch and propped open the screened door and put the bowl on the porch, out of the rain. The rain was still heavy, spilling brutally from clouds that had an underbelly coating as dark as tar. He wondered if James had made it out safely over the slick dirt roads, and he thought of the funeral for Hattie Lewis. He pulled his watch from his shirt pocket and looked at it. It was almost two o'clock, the hour of the funeral. He wondered if it had been postponed. Probably not, he reasoned. Putting off a funeral was like putting off something that was already over. Still, he thought, I'd like for it to be a nice day when I'm buried. I'd like for the sun to be shoveled in with me. He looked across the yard, puddled in water.

Not much of a chance for the dog to be showing up in this kind of weather, he thought.

He was in his chair beside his desk when he heard the whimper on the porch. He got up quickly — too quickly; he could feel the pain in his hip — and went back to the porch and saw the dog standing beside the empty bowl. "Well, I see you made it," he said. "Knew I was by myself, didn't you?" The dog whimpered and stepped to him and lifted her head to his hand.

"Where you been?" he said. "You almost dry. In the well-house? That where you been hiding all this time?" The wellhouse was only a few feet from the porch. "Well, come on in. Keep me company. Won't nobody be out here today." He backed into the kitchen and the dog followed obediently. "Guess maybe you need some water after lapping up that feast," he said. He poured water into a bowl and placed it before the dog and watched her drink. "Wish I had me a camera," he said. "I'd take me a picture of you and prove you're real."

The dog looked up at him and then raised herself on her back legs and placed her front paws on the top brace of the walker between his hands. He laughed in surprise. "I'll be damned," he muttered. He stepped backward cautiously with the walker and the dog stepped with him, holding her paws to the brace. He stepped to the side, and the dog followed. "I'll be damned," he said again. "First time I ever danced with a dog. You sure not proud how you look, are you?" The dog whined an answer.

He kept the dog in the house with him during the afternoon. The dog lay near him, head resting on her outstretched front legs. When he moved, he could sense the dog's eyes following him. He thought: I could lock that dog up in a room and call my daughters and have them come out and prove to them I'm not crazy. But he knew he would not. The dog had the right to be seen or not seen. Besides, now it was a game with his daughters and sons. None of them believed him. They were likely talking to one another on the telephone, saying, "Maybe it's too much for him, living alone like he is. Maybe we ought to check on a home of some kind. Maybe somebody should move in with him."

None of them believed him. It had made him angry; now it amused him.

Late in the afternoon the rain thinned to a mist, and he called Neal Lewis to ask about Hattie's funeral.

"We went ahead with it, Sam," Neal said. "Never saw such a rain. Never in my life. I couldn't even look down in the hole. I knew it was half-full."

"Sorry I couldn't make it over," he said. "Nobody was here to drive me out."

"It was best you didn't," Neal told him. "Old people like us, we don't need to be out in such a rain. But I'm coming over to see you before long, like I said I was."

"I want you to do that, Neal," he said. "Come over for the day."

"You come to see me, too, Sam."

"Maybe I will one of these days," he said.

Kate called before sundown and, minutes later, Carrie called. Both wanted to know if he would have dinner with them. He refused both offers, telling them he was not hungry, but he was, and he decided he would bake fresh biscuits and have biscuits and molasses.

It would not be hard to bake biscuits, he thought. He had sat at the kitchen table hundreds of times and watched her at the cabinet, her hands flashing over the dough, and it did not seem a hard thing to do. He knew the ingredients she used.

He stood at the cabinet and took the wood mixing bowl and scooped three cups of flour from the flour bin, and then he measured out two teaspoons of baking powder and a teaspoon of baking soda and a teaspoon of salt and he mixed it together with his hands. Then he took up a palmful of shortening from the can and dropped it into the middle of the flour mixture, but it did not seem enough and he added another palmful and he began to knead the shortening and flour mixture together, but it was greasy and stuck to his hands.

The dog watched him from the doorway leading into the middle room. "Don't think I know what I'm doing, do you?" he said to the dog. "Think I forgot about the buttermilk, don't you?" He had forgotten, and talking to the dog reminded him. He pulled across the room on his walker and took the buttermilk from the refrigerator and returned to the cabinet and began to pour the milk over the wad of dough. "Ought to be enough," he judged aloud. "Can't be that hard to make biscuits." He kneaded the buttermilk into the shortening-and-flour mixture and the dough became like glue, sticking to his fingers. "Need some more flour," he said profoundly to the dog. The dog tilted her head curiously.

He worked for another thirty minutes with the dough, adding flour and buttermilk and shortening until it caked on his fingers, and then he decided the dough was firm enough and he rolled it out on waxed paper and cut it with the cutter. He had fifty-two biscuits. "Great God," he said in amazement. "I just wanted two or three."

The biscuits were not eatable. They were flat and hard and were colored a murky yellow. He put one in front of the dog and the dog sniffed and looked up at him sadly and trotted away. "Don't know what's good, do you?" he said. He wiped butter across the top of two of the biscuits and poured molasses over them and cut one with his knife and tasted it. He spit the biscuit from his mouth and sat at the table and laughed silently.

She would be laughing, too, he thought. Or scowling. Thinking him an old fool for trying to do something that she had done with ease. Got to get one of the girls to show me how to cook biscuits, he decided. Can't be that hard.

He disposed of the biscuits and cooked an egg with sausage for his supper and an egg for the dog, and was washing the dishes he had used when he saw the light beams from a car striking at the window above the sink. He struggled hurriedly on his walker to the middle room where the dog lay sleeping.

"Come on," he said to the dog. "Go get under the bed." He opened the door to his bedroom and waved, and the dog seemed to understand what he wanted and she trotted quickly to his bed and slipped beneath it. He heard the door to the back porch open.

"Daddy?"

It was Kate.

"In here," he answered.

She came into the middle room, holding a tray of food. "Got you some black-eyed peas and tomato gravy," she said. "Noah said I should bring it out to you."

"You can put it in the stove," he said. "I had some eggs."

She looked at him suspiciously. "You all right?" she asked.

"Don't I look all right?" he said.

"You look fine. But why are you standing there?"

"I was about to go to bed," he said quickly.

"This early? You tired?"

"Thought I'd rest awhile and then watch the TV," he replied.

"Oh," she said. "I'll put this up." She turned to the kitchen and then looked back at him. "Smells like biscuits in here," she said. "Were you cooking biscuits?"

"No. I heated up some you left out here yesterday. They burned a little bit."

"I can bring out some more in the morning."

"Guess maybe it's time I learned how to do it myself. You can come out here and make some and show me how."

"You don't have to cook biscuits, Daddy, or anything. I'm right out the road, and Carrie, too."

"Rather do it myself," he said stiffly.

"Fine," Kate said. "I'll show you how in the morning." She went into the kitchen, and he followed her.

"Didn't see my dog anywhere out there, did you?" he asked.

She tried not to look at him. "No, I didn't," she said.

"Maybe she drowned," he said easily. "Maybe the rain just washed her away."

"How do you know it's a she?" Kate asked.

"She is," he replied. "She's been with me. Props her paws up here on the brace and walks with me. We go dancing. She's a she. I can tell."

"Daddy." There was exasperation in Kate's voice.

He wrote in his journal:

> It rained hard all day, except in the afternoon. I missed
> Hattie Lewis's funeral, but it was too wet to go and
> nobody was here to drive me. But I enjoyed the day, being
> alone most of it. White Dog came in the house and stayed
> with me. She's got good sense for a stray dog. Wouldn't
> touch the biscuits I cooked. I missed Cora today, maybe
> more than any day since she died. I used to like being
> with her when it rained. When we were first married and
> living in Tampa, we would sleep close on days and nights
> when it rained. I loved her deeply.

That night he dreamed of Hattie Lewis, a seventy-year leap across his memory. It was summer, a green day, the sun clear as ice. He was standing alone watching a game of tag in the church yard. The church was almost new. His father had built it.

"Are you playing?" Hattie asked. She had blonde hair with sharp blue eyes that laughed with their own voices.

"No," he said.

"Why not?"

"Just not, that's all."

"Did your daddy build this church? Somebody said he did."

He nodded proudly.

"My daddy said your daddy was dead. Said he died last year. And your mama. She's dead, too, my daddy said."

He nodded again.

"What's it like, your mama and daddy being dead?"

"I—I don't know."

"I wouldn't like it. I'd be sad," she said.

"Uh-huh."

"Did you help your daddy build the church?" she asked.

"I picked up nails."

"Come on and play." She ran off, stopped and looked back at him. "Come on."

"I will in a minute," he said. He looked up at the church his father had built. It was the largest building he had ever seen. It looked cool. He thought he could see his father on a scaffolding, nailing boards. He heard Hattie laugh, saw her dodge the swiping hand of Oscar Beatenbo, saw her hair floating in the green day.

The dream jumped. Another day. Autumn. Colored leaves. Red, gold, brown. Colored leaves ankle deep in the schoolyard. He handed Hattie the comb he had bought for her. She blushed, smiled, her eyes glittering. He could hear Oscar's voice, "Where'd you get that comb, Hattie? Where'd you get it?"

NINE

On the Monday following the rain and Hattie Lewis's funeral, he slept late, and when he awoke he discovered Kate in the kitchen drinking coffee and reading from his Sunday newspaper.

"You ready to learn how to make biscuits?" she asked.

"Can't be that hard," he said.

"Come on and have some coffee and I'll show you," Kate said.

He watched Kate make the biscuits and had her write down in sequence what she had done, and when she left he repeated the sequence and the biscuits were good. He was pleased. Not at all hard to do. He mixed a bowl of milk and fresh biscuits and put it on the steps of the porch for White Dog.

The day was cooler, and he went outside in the late morning and took his hoe from his truck and began to cut away weeds from the nandinas growing at the foundation of his house. He felt rested and strong. The heat of the work surged through his muscles and in his mind he was again young.

He was resting in the shade of a pecan tree when Carrie crossed the lawn from her house.

"Daddy, it's going to get hot out here," Carrie warned. "You know how it gets after it rains and the sun's out. You better not stay out here too long."

"I'm fine. Still cool out."

"It is right now, but you know how it gets when the sun's out," Carrie repeated.

"I don't plan to take root out here," he said. "Just wanted to get rid of some of those weeds while the ground was soft."

Carrie nodded an understanding. She looked sadly at the nandinas. "Mama loved those nandinas," she said softly. "I remember breaking one when I was little. She made me bring one of the limbs to her, and she whipped me with it."

He did not answer.

"Kate said she showed you how to make biscuits," Carrie said.

"I could of done it," he replied. "I thought if one of you didn't show me how, you'd think I was killing myself. Nothing to making biscuits. I used to do it all the time."

"Well, you'll only need a few a day," Carrie said.

"I got my dog to feed," he told her.

"I thought that dog had run off, Daddy."

He looked at Carrie. She had a puzzled, pitying expression on her face. "Run off?" he said. He looked across the yard to the pasture fence. "She's right over yonder, by the fence."

Carrie looked quickly toward his nodding face. She could not see anything. "Daddy, there's no dog over there."

"Well, one of us is blind, and it's not me," he said. He called for the dog. "Come on, girl. Come on."

"Daddy, I don't see nothing."

"My Lord, Carrie, there she comes, plain as day," he exclaimed. He leaned forward over his walker and clapped his hands playfully and pretended that a dog was running toward him. He laughed easily. "Look at that," he said. "Got her paws up on the walker." He rubbed the air at the top brace and cupped an imaginary head in his hands. "That's a good girl. Come on, now, take a step. That's it. That's it." He moved the walker backward and then forward. "You're dancing." He looked at Carrie and beamed. "You ever see a dog dance?"

Carrie's face was ashen. Her mouth tightened at the lips. She stared fearfully at her father. "I — I got to go, Daddy," she whispered.

"You ever see a dog that white, Carrie?"

"I — I got to go."

Carrie turned and walked away rapidly, hugging herself, her head down. He knew what she was thinking: He's crazy. And he knew she would rush to the telephone and call Kate, and the two would weep woefully because their father thought he saw a white dog that could dance with him. And he knew that Carrie and Kate would call their sisters and brothers and say, "We've got to do something. He's getting worse."

He imagined the conversations.

"He's missing Mama and he's making up things."

"Old people get that way."

"He won't go to a doctor. You know he won't."

"I can't stand to see him that way."

The next day, as he worked again outside with his hoe, Kate and Carrie told him they could see White Dog.

"You're right, Daddy, that's the whitest dog I ever saw."

"Can I touch her, Daddy? You think she'd let me touch her?"

"What's the matter with the two of you?" he said. "I don't see no dog."

"Why, right over there, Daddy, down by the barn," Kate said hesitantly.

He knew they had agreed among themselves to humor him, to say they could see the dog. "Guess you must be seeing things," he said. "My dog's in the house, sleeping under my bed." It was the truth, but he knew they would not believe him.

"Well, I — I thought I saw something white," Kate stammered.

"Wadn't my dog," he said firmly, covering a smile. "Might of been a bear. I saw a white bear one time in a circus. Polar bear. They had him sitting in a tub of ice."

Kate stared at her father, then turned her eyes to Carrie, signaling despair.

"How you feeling today, Daddy?" asked Carrie.

"I'm all right," he said.

"You're not lightheaded or anything, are you?" asked Kate.

"Lightheaded?"

"Well, you know what I mean, Daddy," Kate said quickly. "I get that way in this kind of weather."

"Not me," he said. "You get lightheaded, you better go see a doctor."

"Maybe I will," Kate replied. She glanced knowingly at Carrie, then looked away. "As a matter of fact, Daddy, why don't you go in for a checkup with me? It's been a long time since you had one. I can take you tomorrow."

He looked from Kate to Carrie but did not reply.

"There's a new doctor over in Athens, Daddy, and I hear he's really good," Carrie said tentatively. "Mostly he just talks to people. They say he can find out more about a person's health by talking than by poking around over the body."

"Sounds like a head doctor to me," he said.

"He . . . " Kate began, then stopped. She looked at Carrie.

"You think I need a head doctor?" he asked bluntly.

"No, Daddy, that's not it," Carrie whined. "We just thought if you needed to talk to somebody . . . "

"I don't." He could see confusion and fear in the faces of his daughters.

"We just thought we'd ask about a checkup," Kate said quietly.

"I'll think about it," he said.

Carrie looked beyond him, toward the barn. She blurted suddenly, "Daddy, I've got some dog food out at the house. Why don't I bring it out for your dog?"

He could see tears in her eyes. His daughters did not know it was a harmless game that he was playing with them. Someday he would tell them that he had only been pretending, playing with them. Someday they would see White Dog.

In the heat of the late afternoon, he wrote in his journal:
When they were small, I could not play games with my children. There was always work to do. I did not throw baseballs to my sons as other men did. I did not build doll houses for my daughters. There was never enough time. It was sunup-to-sundown work. My children did not know that I had once played games myself. One year I won a contest at the Crimson Clover Festival, climbing the greased flagpole. I was 15, I think (that would have made it 1907). The same year I won a footrace at the county fair. I remember that race because nobody thought I had a chance to win and one of my older brothers (Carl) tried to get me to back out of it. The only person to give me any real competition that day was Horace Brown and I beat him by two steps. He told me later that he had never been beaten

in a footrace and we became friends until his death. I did not run another footrace after that, even with Horace urging me to do so. He said I should try for the Olympics and I used to dream about that. Sometimes when I see the Olympics on the TV, I wonder if I could have made it if I had tried. That would have been something to remember forever. I liked playing baseball in the cow pastures when I was a child. We used dried-up cow droppings to mark off the bases. I was not very good at baseball, however, because I had bad eyes even then. One time I met Ty Cobb and I remember his eyes. They were clear and sharp and I knew that he had been blessed with good vision, which was why he was such a good hitter. But I never wanted to be like Ty Cobb. He turned out mean. The few games that I played, I enjoyed, as all children enjoy play. But I was not a child for long. I had to grow up fast after my father died. Being passed along from house to house of older brothers and other kin, I knew I had to get out on my own. I am now playing a game with my children — especially Kate and Carrie — though I suspect they are not enjoying it. They cannot see White Dog and they think I am making her up. I am at times. Someday, they'll see her and they'll know it was all a game and I can tell them the truth and we'll laugh about it.

TEN

It was now an obsession with the sisters and they talked constantly to one another over the telephone about their father.

Kate: "You know what's going to happen, don't you? Somebody's going to stop in to pay him a visit, to pay their respects because of Mama — somebody like the preacher — and Daddy's going to start bragging about some white dog that's not even there, and it'll get out that he's crazy like old man Bobo Ward. You wait. Every time we go somewhere there'll be people looking at us pitiful-like, like the whole lot of us have lost our senses."

Carrie: "I know it. I keep thinking the same thing. Poor old man Bobo Ward. Last time I saw him he was walking down the road in his long-handle underwear with the bottom unbuttoned and his butt showing. I told you about that. Poor old man. I saw that daughter of his later, up in town. She was in the drugstore buying him some medicine, and I couldn't even look at her, I felt so sorry. When she left, they were saying it took the sheriff to get old man Bobo home. Said he was about to drive everybody in the family up the walls. They just don't know what to do with him."

Kate: "That's what they're going to be saying about us."

Carrie: "At least Daddy's not walking around in his long handles with his butt-flap down."

Kate: "Not now, but he may be before long. I've read stories about how people go crazy. They do it a little bit at a time. One day, it's almost nothing. They're talking along like they always do, and then they start saying things that don't make the first bit of sense, like they were trying to tell a joke, but nothing's funny about it. Next thing you know, they're down on all fours, making out like they're a goat or something."

Carrie: "Oh, Lord, don't say that."

Kate: "Happened that way to that old woman down in Elberton a few years ago. Mama told me about it. Said she was a pillar of the community, even taught school — home economics, Mama said. Then one day they found her on her front porch, in the swing, sitting on a quilt and clucking away like a chicken. Mama said she'd put a dozen eggs on the quilt and was trying to hatch them. Broke every last one of them."

Carrie: "I hope to heaven we won't find Daddy that way, trying to crawl around on all fours, making out like he's a dog."

Kate: "Why'd you say that, Carrie? Oh, Lord, now I'll be worried to death. Maybe that's what's happened — and we don't know it. Maybe he's looking in the mirror and seeing a dog instead of himself. I wish you hadn't said that. I remember reading something about how lots of crazy people get to thinking they're some kind of animal."

Carrie: "I don't even want to talk about it. Makes me want to cry just thinking about it. Every time I think about him patting the air like he was patting a dog's head, saying I was blind because I couldn't see his dog, I can't help but cry."

Kate: "Did Lois call you this morning?"

Carrie: "We talked for a minute. She wanted to know if we'd been able to see the dog yet, and I told her I couldn't even talk about it, it bothered me so much. She sounded put off."

Kate: "I told her the same thing yesterday. I know she thinks we're making it up. I can hear it in her voice. She calls me two or three times a day, like all I've got to do is talk about Daddy."

Carrie: "Sam Junior sounds the same way. He told me last night that we must be making more of it than was needed. Said it may be Daddy's way of keeping everything in balance and we ought not to worry if he wanted to make up having a dog."

Kate: "Well, Sam Junior and Lois and the rest of them don't know what it's like, watching it every day. All they got to do is call up and talk, and a lot of good that does."

Carrie: "I know it."

Kate: "Have you seen Daddy today?"

Carrie: "I was about to go out there."

Kate: "Call me when you get back."

Noah did not mean for the comment to be taken seriously — had said it, in fact, more to tease them than to inspire them — but he knew immediately from their uplifted faces and from the way their eyes flashed with revelation that he had provided them with a plan of action.

"Now, wait a minute," Noah said quickly. "All I said was you ought to put a lookout on your daddy early in the morning. I didn't mean nothing by that. I was just talking."

"What'd you say it again for?" Kate asked indignantly.

"I know that look," Noah told her. "I know you got it in your head. You and Carrie both."

Carrie pushed back the empty coffee cup. Her eyes moistened slightly, and she sniffed softly. She said, "I just came back from watching him sitting out there in his rocking chair with a hairbrush in his hand, brushing thin air, saying he was brushing that white dog's hair. That's what he calls it: White Dog. I couldn't even go back to the house, it scared me so much. I had to come on out here. You ask me, it's a good idea to find out the truth."

"Damn it," Noah sighed. "I don't know why I ever open my mouth around the two of you, especially when Holman's not here to take my side."

"We just want to know if Daddy's going crazy," protested Kate.

"Your daddy's not the one that's crazy. It's the two of you," Noah said bluntly.

"I resent you saying that," Kate replied angrily. "You're not around here in the daytime. You didn't see what Carrie saw."

"I stopped by there on the way in," Noah argued. "Your daddy was sitting in his rocking chair reading the paper. He didn't say nothing about a dog."

"Well, I guess he'd already finished when you got there, Mr. Smartbutt," Kate hissed cynically.

"Good Lord, Kate, don't you know your daddy better'n that? The two of you are aggravating him to death. All he's doing is paying you back. He's putting you on. You know he likes to do that."

"When's he ever done that?" snapped Kate.

Noah stared at Kate in disbelief. "Well, what about last year when he got you going about buying a mule?"

"He was serious about that," Carrie said. "Dead serious. Said he was going to put in his garden with one."

"Come on, Carrie, you know better than that," Noah said. "Mr. Sam can't even walk without using his walker. He knows he can't plow anymore, but he got pure joy out of the two of you fretting over it."

"He drug his plows out," Kate argued.

"He had to make you believe it, didn't he? All he wanted to do was touch them again. The trouble with the two of you is you don't know how a man feels when he can't do something anymore."

"Well, you think what you want to, mister. He was going to buy a mule, before Mama stopped him," Kate said defiantly.

"Your Mama didn't even try to stop him," corrected Noah. "In fact, she said she'd make the call for him. She knew he was putting the two of you on. He's always doing that, and y'all just don't know it."

Carrie rolled her eyes and got up from the kitchen table and poured more coffee into their cups. After a moment, she said, "But the white dog's different, Noah, and you know it."

Noah nodded reluctantly. "I guess that's right. He must think it's there, or he wouldn't've wanted me to kill it."

"But you said it can't be there," Kate said.

"Don't see how," admitted Noah. "Old Red would be barking his fool head off if there was another dog around. Your dogs, too, Carrie."

Carrie sat again at the table. "He keeps saying the dog shows up early every morning to be fed, before we get up and get going."

Kate narrowed her eyes on her sister and said in a low voice, "We could hide out in the ditch, behind that boxwood hedge."

"Good Lord," Noah whispered in desperation.

"You can see the back of the porch clear as day from there," continued Kate.

"If we got out there before sunup, we'd be able to see anything that showed up," Carrie said.

"I don't believe this," Noah moaned. He got up and opened the kitchen door leading to the outside of the house. "I swear, I feel sorry for Mr. Sam. I'm going out to see Holman." He left the house.

"If Daddy sees us, he'll have a fit," Carrie warned.

"He won't see us," promised Kate.

When she left her house the following morning in the soot cloud of night, slipping out the back door, using only the beam of her flashlight, Kate was dressed in jeans and a dark sweater. She had a stocking cap pulled over her hair and the top of her forehead. Her face was smudged with ashes taken from the fireplace. She stood for a moment, letting her eyes adjust to the night, then she raised her flashlight and, partly covering its beam with her fingers, flashed a signal in the direction of Carrie's house. She saw a return light. At least she didn't oversleep, Kate thought. She crouched over and began moving across the lawn, following the familiar path to her father's house.

Carrie was already kneeling behind the boxwood hedge when Kate arrived. Carrie was also dressed in dark clothes, with a stocking cap unfolded down over her hair. She looked at Kate in astonishment.

"What's that you got all over your face?" Carrie whispered.

"Ashes. I got some for you," Kate said. She handed Carrie a small glass jar half-filled with ash.

"I don't want to put that stuff on me," Carrie mumbled.

"Noah said it was what they used to do in the Army. He said it was easy to see a white face from a distance."

"Well, Noah can kiss my foot."

"If Daddy sees you, it won't be a foot-kissing."

"My Lord," sighed Carrie. She opened the jar and dumped the ash out in her hand and rubbed it over her face. "I feel like a fool," she complained. "I hope none of the kids see me like this. They do, they'll be covered up in this stuff."

"It washes off, for crying out loud, Carrie. No reason to take chances. You put up the dogs in the house?"

"I told you I would. You put Red up?"

"Stupid dog didn't even move when I left the house. He was asleep under the kitchen table."

"Is Noah up?" Carrie asked.

"Wadn't when I left, but he was awake. I could tell. He was trying to make me think he was asleep. I could hear him giggling when I left the room."

"Holman was the same," Carrie said. "He thinks we're crazy."

"I don't give a flip what they think," Kate declared in an angry whisper. "It's not their daddy."

"What I say," agreed Carrie. "How long you think we'll have to wait?"

"Don't matter."

"What if he sleeps late?"

"He won't. He went to bed early last night. I saw the lights go out."

"He was hurting some yesterday. Maybe he'll sleep late," Carrie said.

"If he does, we'll come back tomorrow. If he's got a dog, I plan on seeing it."

"Watch out," Carrie said quickly. "That's my foot you're on."

"I thought it was a rock," Kate said.

The two sisters squatted in the ditch behind the boxwood hedge and peered anxiously through the limbs, two dark sentries in the dark of night, and waited for a white dog they did not believe existed. Behind them, in the east, the still-deep frost of morning began to coat the sky.

"He's sleeping late, like I said," Carrie whispered. "It's going to be light before long."

"Let's give him a little more time," Kate said.

A mockingbird began to sing noisily in a nearby tree. A rooster crowed from the farm of Herman Morris, far across the creek on the Goldmine ridge.

And then a light snapped on in Sam Peek's house.

"He's up," Kate said excitedly.

They watched as the bathroom light went on and, a few minutes later, the kitchen light. They could see their father at the kitchen window, hobbling slowly about on his walker.

"He's making biscuits," Kate guessed.

"Looks like it," Carrie said.

They spied impatiently as their father cooked his breakfast and then disappeared from their view to eat. In a few minutes they saw him again at the sink behind the window. They watched him lift something and, turning, make his way across the room. The light to the back porch snapped on. They heard a door open and saw him at the steps of the porch, bending to place a bowl on the steps. They heard his soft voice: "Come on, girl. Breakfast time."

"Oh, my Lord," Carrie said in a soft whine. She bit her lip to stop the surge of pity.

"Ssssssh," Kate commanded. She moved closer to the hedge and pushed aside a boxwood limb.

"You see anything?" Carrie asked.

"Nothing yet," answered Kate.

Suddenly, from behind them, a dog barked sharply.

"Good Lord," Kate exclaimed, leaping to her feet.

A short, shrill scream spit from Carrie's throat. She grabbed Kate.

The dog sprinted across the road, barking happily, wagging his tail. He nudged playfully against Kate.

"Red," Kate said angrily. "How did you get —?" She heard a roll of laughter from beneath the black canopy of a pecan tree.

"Noah," Carrie snapped. "And Holman."

"Damn you, Noah," Kate yelled.

From across the yard, Sam Peek called, "What's going on out there?"

"Daddy," Carrie whispered fearfully. She dropped to her knees below the hedge. Kate dropped beside her.

"Who's out there?" he called again.

Noah and Holman stepped from the shadows of the pecan tree.

"It's just us, Mr. Sam," Noah said in a loud voice.

"Who?"

"Noah and Holman," Noah said again. He paused and smiled at the hiding Kate and Carrie. "And the girls," he added cheerfully.

"What're you doing?"

"The girls were out taking a walk," Noah called back. He began to laugh uncontrollably.

"Yes sir," Holman sang out. "The girls were out taking a walk and — and me and Noah heard a dog barking and we came out looking for them." He laughed hard, bending over, swallowing the sound.

"Where're the girls?" he asked harshly.

"Right here," Noah said.

"I don't see them," he said.

Kate and Carrie stood slowly. They glared at their husbands.

"Right here, Daddy," Kate called. She held the flashlight up.

"Here, Daddy," echoed Carrie.

"Come on up here," their father ordered.

"Damn," Kate muttered. She turned to Noah. "I'll get you for this if it takes the last breath in my body, Noah," she sputtered in a low, menacing voice.

"Come on, Kate," Carrie said.

He watched his daughters approach the house, followed by Noah and Holman. His daughters looked absurd, dressed in dark clothing, their heads covered with stocking caps, their faces smudged.

"Good God," he said. "What're you doing out this time of morning, looking like that?"

His daughters stood sheepishly before him, their faces lowered in shame.

"Well, like I said," Noah replied confidently, "the girls got it in their heads they ought to be out walking for exercise. There was something on television about it a couple of nights ago." He turned to Holman. "That's when it was, wadn't it, Holman?"

"Seems to me that's right," Holman said. A smile broke in his face like a light. He turned away.

"Anyway, it said early morning was the best time of day for it. We tried to talk them out of it, but you know how they can get, Mr. Sam."

"What's that you got all over your face?" he asked suspiciously.

"Uh," Kate muttered.

"Ah, it's —" Carrie said.

"Well, that's our doing, Mr. Sam," Noah said quickly. "Me and Holman were just pulling their legs. Told them it'd keep the bugs off them. All it is, is fireplace ashes."

"Good God," he said sorrowfully. He looked at his daughters and shook his head.

"It was Holman and Noah, Daddy," Carrie said defensively. "They were just trying to scare us. We were just — just walking."

"You want to walk, you do it in the daytime, so you can be

seen," he said. "I could of shot you."

"Yes sir," Carrie whined.

"Probably scared off my dog, with all that racket," he said. "She likes to eat this time of morning."

Kate could feel tears welling in her eyes. It was sad, watching him like that, standing in the porch light, leaning heavily on his walker, looking for an imaginary dog. "We'll go home now, Daddy," she said. Then: "We won't walk any more this time of the morning."

He did not see his daughters for the rest of the day. The day was warm and clear, and he went out among his pecan trees for a short time before retiring to his padded rocking chair to rest his aching hip. At lunch he made a peanut butter sandwich and ate it and then went to the front porch to sit and watch for his white dog. The dog had been driven away, he believed, by the early-morning nonsense of his daughters. It didn't matter. She was not gone, only hiding.

In the afternoon, he napped fitfully, dreaming a nightmarish dream of his daughters wandering ethereally in their strange dress, with gray-black faces like mourners. When he awoke, the pain in his hip had increased, and he took aspirin. In early evening, he went to the front door and called for the white dog, and the dog appeared out of the tangle of the shrubbery and trotted into the house.

"Been keeping out of sight, have you?" he said to the dog. "Don't blame you. You ought to be hiding from some folks." He thought of his daughters and smiled. "Lord, they're enough to hide from sometimes."

He fed his dog and watched television and then went into the middle room to sit at his desk and write in his journal.

> *Not much to say today. Kate and Carrie caused a ruckus this morning by wanting to get out and go walking when it was still dark. Noah and Holman made a joke of it but I could tell Kate and Carrie did not think it was funny. They were both spirited children and they still are. Sometimes I think they have too much spirit. My hip has hurt worse today than it has in a long time. I fixed White Dog some food, but didn't eat much myself. I hope I sleep tonight.*

ELEVEN

It was after midnight, and he was awake, sitting in his padded rocker beside his roll-top desk. The pain in his hip nauseated him. He had taken the druggist's medicine earlier, but the pain was still very great, and he could not rest. He had not moved for hours, not since he had taken his journal from his desk to write in. His mouth was dry. He wanted water, but knew he could not rise from his chair and pull himself into the kitchen. He breathed in a shallow sucking through his opened lips. A film of perspiration coated his forehead.

He could hear from the living room the steady sizzling of the television, which he had left on when he went to take the medicine. He had listened to the faint playing of The Star-Spangled Banner at sign-off and had imagined the black-and-white fluttering of images across the screen — a formation of jet airplanes, soaring upward in perfect symmetry, splitting and backdiving gracefully into the clear, endless ocean of the sky. And the flag superimposed over the airplanes, the flag rippling in a wind of music, its sharp-pointed stars dancing across the cloth.

Should have turned it off, he thought. It'll be on all night. But he had meant to return to the living room and to the television shows he enjoyed. "Bonanza." He had wanted to see "Bonanza." He liked Ben Cartwright and he liked Hoss, but he didn't think much of Little Joe and Adam. Little Joe and Adam seemed put-ons to him. But not Hoss. Hoss had the heart of an innocent, a large, playful man who believed in being right and doing right. Hoss was the kind of man everyone ought to be, he believed.

She had liked "Bonanza" also. She saw in Hoss and Little Joe and Adam likenesses of her own sons. Sometimes she would say,

"That's just like . . ." and she would name one of her sons. Always, when she found the comparison, Hoss or Little Joe or Adam had done something heroic. And she had liked Sid Caesar and Milton Berle. They made her laugh. And she had liked to hear Dennis Day sing. His soft Irish ballads made her weep. Her sons were also like Dennis Day.

The sizzling of the television was like the sound of burning green wood.

I'm wrong, he thought. "Bonanza's" not on tonight.

What is tonight? he asked silently.

Thursday, he answered silently.

No. Not Thursday.

Wednesday.

What was the date of his journal?

Friday?

He could feel the burning from his hip seeping into his body, spiraling through him, rising into his stomach and throat, and he began to weep from the pain and from the realization that he was alone.

He thought of her. When she was there, she would sit near him with a book she pretended to read, watching his face for the signals of hurt.

"You want water?"

"A little bit. My throat's dry."

"Better take another pill."

"What time was it when I took the last one?"

"It's been a couple of hours. You can take another one now."

But she was not there, and he could not get the water or the pills.

He felt White Dog move against his chair and nuzzle her face gently into his arm. If you want out, you'll have to get out by yourself, he thought. He leaned his head against his chair and smiled at the absurd image of White Dog opening a door with her paws and strolling outside. But maybe it was possible. Some animals were smarter than people. He remembered a mule he had owned: Bell. Bell was smart. There was not a gate lock Bell could not open, given time, or a fence Bell could not leap. In spring, in the time for plowing, Bell would tease him by escaping from the pasture at night and he would have to go into the swamp in the mornings and play hide-and-seek until Bell surrendered. In his mind, he could see Bell slowly circling the thicket of swamp brush, watching him. Great God Almighty, Bell could jump. Not a horse alive could jump fences better. But mules were smart. Smarter than horses.

The pain was in his mouth, his face, behind his eyes. He sucked hard to breathe. A trickle of perspiration seeped from his forehead, down the slope of his nose and into his eye. He moaned aloud and White Dog rubbed against his arm.

He knew he would have to get the pill and take it. Maybe the pill would break open inside him and spread its numbing anesthesia to his brain, and he would rest. He pulled his foot from the lower brace of the walker, where he had rested it to stop the aching in his hip. A surge of blood pumped through him, slamming against the thin shell of his chest. He swallowed to control the nausea. White Dog stepped back from him and whined. Don't get in the way, he thought. You get in my way, I'll fall for sure. He caught the hand support of his walker and eased himself forward from his seat. The pain raged in his body. There was no strength in his arms or legs and he paused and bowed his head and waited for the pain to subside. He could feel in his lips the pulse of his heartbeat. He had never felt as weak. Got to get the pill, he thought. Got to.

He pulled harder at the hand support and his body rose up slowly from the chair. Lights exploded in his eyes, flashing in colors. Perspiration oozed from his face, across the corners of his mouth. A fire was in his hip. White Dog lifted her front feet and placed them on the bar of the walker. He tried to speak, to push the dog away, but he could not make words. He stood on his good leg and lifted the walker and slipped it forward and White Dog dropped from the bar and moved away. He limped once on his good leg, sliding the walker. He could sense a queasiness rising sourly from his stomach, and he tried to swallow it back, but it filled his mouth and spilled over his chin and onto his chest. He coughed, and the walker slid from his hands and he fell violently across the floor. He cried aloud, cried in great hurt, and the pain crushed him, squeezed his mind into unconsciousness.

Kate awoke suddenly, jerked from sleep by intuition violent in its power. She touched Noah, and Noah rolled sleepily from his side to his back.

"What's the matter?" Noah asked.

"I don't know."

"You hear something?"

"I'm not sure."

Noah listened. "I don't hear anything," he said. "Nothing."

"Something's wrong," Kate said. "Get up and see what it is."

"Good Lord, Kate." Noah did not move. The gathering of the thin curtain billowed easily at the opened window of their bedroom.

"Well, if you won't, I will," complained Kate. She slipped from the bed and went to the window and looked out. She could see the lights from her father's house. "What time is it?" she asked.

Noah turned the clock on the bedside stand to him. "One," he said. "A few minutes after."

"Daddy's up."

Noah could hear the fretting of her voice. He moved from the bed and stood beside her at the window. "Maybe he's just using the bathroom."

"Too many lights on," Kate mumbled. "Maybe he's sick."

"Maybe," Noah said. He pushed back the curtain of the window and peered into the murkiness of the night. Then: "God Almighty." His voice was a whisper.

"What is it?" Kate asked.

"Out there."

"What?"

"Look." He pointed with his finger. White Dog stood at the side of the road, leading to the house, her head majestically lifted.

Kate's hands flew to her face. "The white dog," she gasped. "Daddy was right. It's there." She shuddered suddenly. "Noah, something's wrong." She touched her own arm with her hand. Her arm was cold. She shuddered again. She could sense her father's voice clinging to her like air. She said again, in a loud cry, "Noah, something's wrong."

And Noah, too, shuddered. "I'll go see." He quickly pulled on his pants and started out of the room. "Call Carrie," he said. "Tell Holman to come on out."

"I'm going, too," Kate insisted.

"Call Carrie first, then come on," Noah said. He rushed from the room.

Noah did not see the white dog, but it did not matter. The white dog had been there. He had seen it. And Kate had seen it. There was something eerie about seeing the white dog standing motionless at the roadside. As he ran across the yard to his father-in-law's house, Noah could feel the chill still clamped to him. Where in the name of hell had the dog been all this time? he wondered. How could a dog keep out of sight so well? God, it was white, the whitest animal he'd ever seen, and he'd killed a white deer on a hunt to Little St. Simon's Island.

Noah saw the lights snap on in the house where Carrie and Holman lived. Yes, he thought, something's wrong. Bad wrong. He ran faster. He saw the white dog again as he crossed the road. The dog was standing on the steps of the back porch, its head bobbing at the door in a sniffing motion. And then the dog turned its head to him and moved slowly from the steps and disappeared into the shrubbery beside the house. "Damn," Noah muttered. The dog frightened him.

Noah did not think his father-in-law was alive when he saw him in the floor, his walker toppled across his body. He threw the walker aside and fell on his knees and turned his father-in-law and saw the thick, clabbered waste on his face and chest. The odor struck Noah forcefully, and he gagged. He cupped his hand and wiped the waste away from his father-in-law's mouth and he tried to feel for a neck-pulse. The pulsebeat was weak and erratic. "Oh, God," Noah whispered. He heard the screened door to the back porch open and the rush of footsteps through the kitchen. He knew it was Kate.

"Daddy?" Kate cried from the kitchen.

"In here," Noah said.

Kate hurried into the room and saw Noah holding her father.

She stopped abruptly and stared down at them. She stepped backward, as though pushed. She said, in a small, frightened voice, "Is — is he . . . ?"

"No," Noah snapped. "Call out to Holman and tell him to bring his car, then get me a wet cloth."

"He's — he's dead?"

"No, damn it. Do what I tell you," Noah growled. "We've got to get him to the hospital."

TWELVE

The sweet, numbing medicine flowed in the rivers of his blood stream, and he was euphoric.

He did not know he was in a hospital bed or that a slender plastic tube curled down from a container above him and fit into his arm, slow-dripping the sweet, numbing medicine into him. He did not seem to be at all fixed to a place or an object. He seemed, instead, to float weightlessly in the thin ether of a dream, with the power of gods to push himself about in flight. And in swim strokes, his arms pulling him easily through cool, astral distances, he soared freely above his daughters and sons, who waited as sentinels at his bedside.

His dream was as sweet as his medicine.

Marshall Harris asked, "You going to marry Cora?"

"Would if I had some money," he said.

"Sam, you wait on money, the only way you'll be taking that woman to bed is in your sleep and I'll guarantee you that ain't as good as the real thing."

"Lot you know about it," he snorted. "Don't see you knocking down the doors of any women around here."

Marshall laughed. "What you see and what you don't see are two different things. I do all right."

"Maybe she wouldn't marry me if I asked her," he said. "She's got her mind set on being a nurse."

"Sam, you're about as blind as that old colored man that plays the guitar up by the courthouse," Marshall countered. "Never saw a woman that wanted to be married as much as Cora. Looks to me like the only person she wants to play nurse to is you."

"I don't know —"

"Well, I do," Marshall said. "Every time I see her, she's asking where you are. I swear to God, it looks like you think more of them mules down in the stables than you do her. You spend more time with them."

"I got work to do, Marshall."

"You plowing the wrong fields, Sam. The wrong fields. That's one good-looking woman."

He stroked his arms through the ether and turned in his flight like an eagle skimming across currents of warm, billowing air and he was in bed with her, holding her, and she was fitting her body gladly to him. Her face was against his face, damp-hot in the dark, damp-hot room. There was a sound, as soft as purring, in her throat. She moved quickly and raised her body over him, her face thrown back in a swallowed cry. The pink nipple tongues of her breasts were moist and slippery. She was beautiful. Slender and muscled and graceful. She was beautiful beyond all beauty he had ever imagined. And he bridged his hard, strong body against her, effortlessly lifting her with his thighs and abdomen, and the swallowed cry flew like a song from her throat.

He stroked again with his arms — powerfully — and now he was standing on the roadside with her as she coaxed the uncertain white puppy to her.

"It's all right," she said. "I won't hurt you." She turned her face to him. "Looks starved. We need to find it some food."

"Somebody threw it out," he said. "Looks like they just opened a car door and threw it out."

"It'll die out here."

"I guess. It's not very old."

"I'm going to take it home."

"I don't know —"

"I do."

He twisted his body and flipped his hands gently and felt the cool air of his dream sliding through his fingers. His fingers touched the face of White Dog. White Dog stood with her front feet on the brace of his walker.

"You want out, you'll have to let yourself out," he said. "I can't move."

White Dog stepped back, still on her back legs, standing as erect as a man. She turned and walked on her back legs to the kitchen door and turned the knob with her paw and pushed open the door and walked outside.

He laughed, watching White Dog. He said, "Great God Almighty. Nobody believes I've got a white dog. And she can dance with me and walk on her hind legs and open doors."

"Daddy?"

He opened his eyes. He could smell the disinfectant of the hospital.

"Daddy? It's me. Alma."

He nodded. the faces of his other children crowded in the periphery of his vision.

"How do you feel?" asked Alma.

He was tired, but he did not hurt. He saw the coil of the slender plastic tube. "All right," he said hoarsely.

"You've got an infection in your hip," Alma told him. "They're giving you antibiotics. I guess you passed out from the pain."

"I slipped," he said weakly.

Kate moved beside Alma. She said, eagerly, "Daddy, we saw the white dog."

He heard her voice from the hallway of the hospital, a lunatic squawking that pierced the thickness of the walls and echoed in a shrill, annoying pitch. Neelie.

Good God, he thought: Neelie.

She entered the room with Kate, pushing past Kate in an exaggerated rush that carried her dramatically to his bedside. She clasped her hands nervously, in a praying motion, and let them tremble beneath her chin. Her eyes dampened instantly. "Oh, Jesus, Lord, you doing all right, Mr. Sam?" Neelie cried.

"I'm all right, Neelie," he said calmly. He could see Kate behind Neelie, rolling her eyes upward, mumbling to herself.

"They told me you done almost drown in your own puke," Neelie wailed.

Kate sighed aloud.

"Don't think so," he said. He wanted to laugh at Kate.

"Jesus, Lord, don't know why them girls didn't call Neelie soon as it happened," Neelie complained. "Them girls don't think right, Mr. Sam."

"I called you the next day, Neelie," Kate said defensively. Neelie turned to acknowledge Kate. "I know you did, honey," she said pitifully. "You one of the sweet ones, thinking about Neelie."

Kate moved close to the bed. Her face was splotched from aggravation. "You feeling better, Daddy?"

"Honey, he feeling fine," Neelie said authoritatively. "Got him some color. He feeling fine."

"I'm better," he said. "Not much pain in my hip."

"Neelie insisted on coming to see you," Kate told him. "We left Carrie cleaning the house and watching the kids."

"Them's two sweet girls," Neelie declared. "They always helping Neelie out. I been trying to get up here, but Arlie's been off working a sawmill job up near Gainesville, leaving me with all them babies. Jesus, Lord, them babies keep Neelie on the go."

"It's all right," he said. "I'm glad you could come today."

"Well, you quit your worrying," Neelie commanded. "We getting things ready for you down at the house. Bless them sweet girls. They been helping Neelie out a little."

Kate rolled her eyes again, wearily.

"It's a good thing you around, Neelie," he said. "I noticed they work better when you're there with them, setting a good example."

Kate glared at him.

"They good girls."

"They are. Yes, they are," he said.

"They just ain't never had it hard, like we did, Mr. Sam."

"I guess not."

"Ain't their fault. Neelie's been doing for them since they was babies. They used to it."

Kate looked away. He knew she was chewing on her lower lip, her habit of frustration.

"You been feeding my dog?" he asked Kate.

"We put some food out every night and it's gone the next morning," Kate said. "I guess it's your dog. Nobody's seen it since the other night."

"Can't nobody see my dog unless she wants you to," he said smugly.

Neelie leaned close to him. She whispered, "That a ghost dog, ain't it?"

"Might be," he said.

"The girls told me about that dog. Say it's white."

"What I call her. White Dog."

"Kate say she seen it."

"I did," Kate said evenly. "Noah saw it, too. Noah found where it'd been staying, Daddy. Under the house, right under where your bed is."

He moved against the pillow on his bed. He could see the apprehension in Neelie's eyes. "Maybe you saw her, or maybe you just thought you did. Sometimes when I'm playing with her, she just turns her head and she's gone."

Neelie moaned fearfully.

"Daddy's just putting you on," Kate said. "It's a real dog. I saw it. Noah, too."

"Just disappears, like it never was there."

"Daddy, don't do that. You'll scare Neelie."

Neelie touched Kate's arm. "Honey, you don't know about ghost dogs. I seen two or three. Don't never bark. Don't no dogs bark around it, neither." Her voice trembled.

Funny, he thought. I've never heard White Dog bark. Never. Whimper, yes. But not bark. And I've never heard any other dogs barking because White Dog was around. He forced a short laugh. "Nothing but a stray," he said. "Somebody must of had her tied up and beat on her. She's scared of people. Everybody but me. That's what you get for feeding a stray."

"I don't want nothing to do with that dog," Neelie said.

"Neelie, that dog doesn't want anything to do with you either, or nobody else for that matter," Kate said. "God knows where she stays, but she keeps away from everybody but Daddy."

"You'll see her," he promised. "Soon as I get home, you'll see her. I'll get her to come out. You'll see her dancing with me on my walker."

"I don't want nothing to do with that dog," Neelie said again.

Two days later, Kate and Carrie drove him to his home.

"You need to get inside and get some rest," Carrie suggested as she helped him from the car.

"I will in a minute," he said. "I want to see my dog."

"Daddy, that dog's not going to show itself," Kate said. "Not with us around."

"Go on inside then," he said. "You can look from the window."

"Come on, Daddy, you need to get in. It's hot out here."

"Not to I see my dog."

His daughters looked at one another in resignation. They knew it was useless to argue. Carrie picked up his suitcase and walked into the house and Kate followed.

He hobbled on his walker to the edge of the yard. The infection in his hip had been washed clean by the dripping antibiotics, and there was only the pain of his weight, but it was a familiar pain. He stood at the yard's edge and called, "Come on, girl. Come on out." He saw a movement at the barn, and White Dog stepped from the shadow of a shed where he stored farm equipment. She lifted her head suspiciously and watched him.

He began to hobble-walk toward the dog, talking to her. "You miss me, girl? Wouldn't let them see you, would you? They think you're a ghost. Come on. It's all right."

The dog hesitated and he stopped walking and reached into his coat pocket and pulled out a paper napkin. He unfolded it ceremoniously and held up a biscuit. "Hospital bread," he said. "Not as good as mine, but it's bread. Come on, girl."

The dog trotted to him, her head down. She stopped before the walker and rose up gracefully and placed her front feet on the top brace. He touched her face, stroking it gently, then gave her the biscuit. "All right, let's dance," he said playfully. He balanced on his good leg and began to move the walker slowly to the side and then back. The dog moved with him. He laughed.

Inside the house, her face pressed comically to the window of his bedroom, Carrie whispered in awe, "My God. Look at that."

"I told you," Kate said softly. "I told you."

"He was right," Carrie said. "Look. They're dancing. That's what it looks like — dancing."

In the weeks that followed, his children and his grandchildren began to see White Dog, but always at a distance, always as something secretive, something poised to leap away and disappear. They could not touch her. They called and coaxed and bribed with food held in their hands, but White Dog would not approach them.

"My dog," he said to his children and his grandchildren, stressing the My, "won't have nothing to do with nobody but me."

"Jesus, Lord," Neelie said in astonishment. "That dog ain't real, Mr. Sam. Never seen a dog like that. Slinking around, like it was part snake. I seen her down by the barn. Clapped my hands at her, and she drop down on her belly and slink off. That dog ain't real. Look like a ghost, like I been saying it was. Looks to me like it'd get some dirt on it, being white like it is."

"She takes a bath every night, Neelie."

"She what?"

"Takes her a bath every night," he said seriously. "Goes in the bathroom and runs her a tub of water and takes a bath."

Neelie laughed nervously. "You like putting Neelie on, don't you, Mr. Sam?" But Neelie was suspicious of White Dog. On the days that she came to the house, to supervise Kate and Carrie and the other daughters if the other daughters were visiting, she looked cautiously for White Dog. He had seen Neelie outside, holding a stick, wagging it menacingly, as though warding off evil spirits, and he had heard her shrill, loud voice talking to the empty space about her: "Get on from me, you ghost dog. Don't you go putting them ghost eyes on Neelie." Once he brushed out White Dog's hair and took the pulled-out threads of hair and rolled them in a ball and gave them to Neelie, telling her it was an antidote against White Dog's power. Neelie pushed the ball of hair into her dress pocket and swore she would never harm White Dog. "That ghost dog's done come to be around you, Mr. Sam," she prophesied.

"Neelie, that dog's just a dog," he said to her. "Somebody must of beat it when it was little. I fed her, and she just took up with me. She just trusts me. I was just teasing you about that hair ball."

"You say what you want, Mr. Sam. I know ghost eyes when I look at ghost eyes. I'll be keeping that hair ball."

At night, when he was alone, White Dog lay on the floor beside his chair. He liked talking to her, liked the way her ears lifted to his voice, liked the gaze of her eyes.

"You're not a ghost, are you?" he said to the dog. "No, you're not a ghost."

Still, he thought, it was curious that he had never heard White Dog bark.

And there was something else: he did not know how White Dog got out of the house on the night that he fell from his walker. He had closed all of the doors. He remembered it. He remembered clearly. Because of Neelie's talk about the Morris boys, he had closed the doors.

THIRTEEN

In early July, he began to go often in his truck to visit the cemetery where his wife and his son were buried, and the dog would follow him, a magnificent white blur racing across fields and along the roadside. The dog knew where he was going in his clattering truck and would race ahead and be waiting for him at the cemetery, hidden among the shrubbery of the hedgerow.

It pleased him that the dog was attentive. He kept biscuits in his coat pockets and he would call the dog to him and feed her before going to the gravesite. The dog would wait beneath the shrubbery, watching him, and when he hobbled back to his truck, the dog would move from the shrubbery and go to him and rise up with her front paws on the walker.

"Go home," he would say, stroking her face. "I'll see you there." And the dog would turn and retreat to the hedgerow and watch as he climbed awkwardly into his truck. When she heard the truck motor, the dog would leap into the road and sprint across the cemetery and across the field, running powerfully ahead of him. He would watch the dog from his slow-following truck, marveling at the speed and the beauty of the speed. "Great God," he would whisper to himself.

He went often to the cemetery because he believed it was where he belonged. At the cemetery the memories he wished to experience were vivid and lasting, not like the dream fragments that struck him in sleep and vanished half-finished and worrisome. At the cemetery he thought of being young, and with her, and those were the best of his memories.

Autumn, 1915.

"Who's that girl?" he asked Marshall Harris.

"Where?" Marshall said.

"Over there." He motioned with his head across the crowd gathered on the lawn in front of the cafeteria, and Marshall followed the nod with his eyes.

"Don't know. Never saw her before," Marshall said. "Nice looking. Got kind of a big nose, though. She's new. Guess this is her first year."

He was twenty-three and the superintendent of farms at the Madison Agricultural and Mechanical School. He had been shy in the presence of girls since Hattie Carey, though he had dated occasionally and had even considered marrying a woman he met in Athens. The woman was older and demanding, and he had walked away during an argument and did not return to her. It was, he later believed, a fortunate escape. But the girl across the lawn from him was appealing. Marshall was right, he thought; her nose was large, but not distracting.

"Go on," Marshall urged. "Go over there and introduce yourself. Tell her you run this place. She'll be impressed."

He shook his head and smiled foolishly. "Never been good at that," he admitted.

"Well, it don't bother me none," Marshall said. "You wait right here."

He watched as Marshall pushed his way through the crowd and approached the girl. He saw her smile and speak politely, and then he saw her face furrow inquisitively, and the smile broadened. Marshall turned and pointed toward him. He saw her rise on tiptoe and search across the crowd. And then she saw him. She smiled and, he thought, blushed. He was not sure if she blushed, but it seemed so. She looked at Marshall and then back to him. Marshall was talking, making exaggerated motions with his hands, and he knew that Marshall was telling grand lies. He saw her laugh quickly, thought he heard the laugh. Marshall waved to him in a beckoning motion. He waved back and slowly moved toward Marshall and the girl.

"This is Robert Samuel Peek," Marshall said seriously, when he approached, "but everybody just calls him Sam."

The girl smiled shyly. She was shorter than he thought from across the lawn. "Hello," he said timidly.

"And this is my friend — uh, what was it?" Marshall said.

"Cora," she replied.

"That's right. Cora. Cora, ah —"

"Wills," she said.

"Cora Wills," Marshall declared. "She's a nurse, Sam."

"I want to be," Cora Wills corrected.

"Well, Sam, here, he owns all the land this school's on," Marshall said.

He laughed, surprising himself, and Cora Wills also laughed.

"No, I mean it," Marshall continued. "I'm one of the hired hands that help keep the place up."

"Only land I own is what's on the bottom of my shoes," he said.

"Well, I got to go now," Marshall announced. "Leave you two alone. You can name your first baby after me." He walked away, laughing merrily.

Marshall Harris was also a memory.

Marshall had been a brilliant student of Latin. On the day that he married Cora Elizabeth Wills, Marshall handed him a sheet of paper containing the phrase, *amicus usque ad aras*.

"What's that supposed to mean?" he asked Marshall.

"It means 'A friend as far as to the altars,'" Marshall said. "And that's as far as I'm following you, Sam. You got to do the rest on your own, if you know what to do."

Marshall had wanted to be a pharmacist, but he was killed in World War One, in France. He had volunteered, he said boastfully, to protect his good friends Sam and Cora Peek and their first child, who would be named Marshall. Once, after the news of Marshall's death, he looked up the phrase *amicus usque ad aras* in a book of Latin. The phrase also meant "A friend to the last extremity."

He was sad that he had not named a child for Marshall Harris.

He went often to the cemetery, and he spent long hours writing in his journal. His journal was important. Writing in it became a ritual to ward off the silence that was suddenly around him. He did not write only to tell his daily stories, but to read, at later times and in lonely hours, what he had written, to remember that on exact days, exact events had happened. And his journal filled with words.

July 2, 1973
Four or five of the grandkids were down today. They were all out watching the eclipse of the sun, which lasted for several minutes. They tried to get me out to see it, but I stayed in. No need to take a chance on ruining what little sight I've got left. I guess if I was young like they are, I'd be looking. It's a rare thing that happens, like Halley's Comet. The big news today other than the eclipse is that Congress approved an increase in Social Security benefits. A little more than 5 percent. We can use it, the way things cost.

July 3, 1973
I saw a picture on the TV about Charles Lindbergh flying across the Atlantic in 1927. Of all the things that have happened in my life, that was the one thing that stands out. Lindbergh did it by himself in a little airplane with one motor. He didn't know where he was most of the time. I liked the picture. Seeing how people looked in those days reminded me how things have changed. It also made me realize how old I am. I was born before the automobile and the airplane and a long time before radio and TV. I guess someday people will fly around in space like they drive around in automobiles, but I won't be one of them. I wouldn't even get in Charles Lindbergh's Spirit of St. Louis *if it was tied to the ground with the motor off. Carrie called today to say she had a touch of the flu. If Cora was still alive she would want to call the doctor. She always worried about Carrie. Tomorrow is the 4th, Independence Day.*

July 10, 1973
A man selling hearing aids came by the house today. He said he just making a "cold call," but I suspect Kate and Carrie are behind it. They think I'm going deaf. I let him test me. He said I'd lost half of my hearing and I ought to buy one of his hearing

devices. I told him I was eighty years old, which meant I'd lost one-quarter of my hearing every 40 years. At that rate I'd be 160 before I went completely deaf. He left without a sale. I think I'll buy one of those hearing horns to stick up to my ear when Kate and Carrie come out. I heard on the radio that Richard Nixon might have to resign because of that Watergate scandal. He ought to. The way he looks he reminds me of Calvin Coolidge and I never liked Coolidge. I read a story in the newspaper today about Betty Grable, who died on July 2. She was a pretty woman. She was married to Harry James from Macon, Georgia. I forgot to include it in my journal on that date.

July 13, 1973

My hip hurt more than usual today and I stayed inside with White Dog and took a long nap. I dreamed as I always do now. In my dream I was at the University of Georgia and a bunch of us boys were thrown off the freight train we used to hook rides on. It was true enough. We did get thrown off a freight train. Some of the boys got up a plan to get even with the train engineer. There was a bridge over the railroad track and a big curve in the track coming out from under the bridge. The engineer always had to slow down and stick his head out of the side of the engine to see what was ahead. Some of the boys got on that bridge and when the train came along below them and the engineer stuck his head out, they peed on him from the bridge. I won't say I did any of the peeing, but I was there. I don't know where dreams come from. I guess if a person's old enough they just seep out of things that have happened that the mind keeps stored away. Kate and Noah went to town to get me some more medicine from the drug store and the pain has eased. The trouble is, I'm not sleepy now. I got a letter from Paul and Sam, Jr. today. They both sent church bulletins. Paul preached a sermon last week called Good Hats a Quarter; God Hates a Quitter. Sounds interesting.

July 17, 1973

Lightning struck one of the pecan trees in the flat today and split a limb off. I could see the smoke coming off the limb from the living room window. They say lightning won't strike in the same place twice, but it does. It has hit in the flat many times over the years. There must be something in the ground, maybe iron ore, that attracts it. Cora was always afraid of lightning. One time in Tampa I came home in a storm and found her hiding in a corner with a quilt over her. I always think of her when it storms now. Maybe it's the rain and the wind or the way it gets dark, but storms leave me lonely. I haven't heard from James in a couple of weeks. He doesn't write as much as the others, but he's good about calling. If I don't hear by the weekend I'll get Kate to give him a call to make sure he's all right. With the rain, I did not go to the cemetery today as I had planned. A news report today said Nixon's popularity was on the way down. I guessed it would be since they found out about the secret recordings he made in the Oval Office.

July 19, 1973

It was in the paper that the Vietnam War may soon be over. I can only say thank God. I never understood why we were in that war. I almost went to World War One, but my lottery number didn't come up. It was supposed to be the war to end all wars, but I don't think war will ever end. Man likes killing. Marshall Harris was killed in World War One. He was a good friend at Madison, maybe the best friend I ever had. I remember Uncle Zack talking about the Civil War. I was just a boy, but the way Uncle Zack talked the war was still going on. He came back from the war shell shocked. He used to saw away on an old fiddle, saying he was playing different tunes, but it was the same noise every time. They would hide his fiddle, but he always seemed to find it. Maybe there won't be another war for a few years. I stayed worried when James was in Thailand, before all the fighting started in Vietnam. Everybody but me thought he was in Hawaii. He told me where he was in case anything happened to him. I used to stay awake at night thinking about him. But he's safe. I saw Hugh Carter not long ago. His boy was killed in Vietnam. I got my bill from the drug store today and it was higher than last time. Somebody's making a killing off keeping people alive.

July 22, 1973

Clete Walton, who is the sheriff, stopped by to ask me if I had seen any cows on the loose lately. I told him I saw Pete Morris driving a couple across the field on the old Vandiver place. Pete is one of the Morris boys that Neelie's boy hangs around with. I didn't ask Clete why he wanted to know about cows. He is the sheriff and his business is his business. My brother Carl was once the chief of police of Hartwell. I don't know it to be true, but there's a story about Carl taking a gun away from a colored man who had killed somebody in a fight over a game of cards. Carl walked right up to the man with the man aiming a gun at his face and took it away. Maybe Pete was stealing cows. Neelie's right about those boys. That's a sorry lot. I would think about locking my doors at night if I had any locks on them. I wonder if White Dog would attack anybody that tried to get in. I doubt it. She seems to be afraid of everybody but me. I got a letter from Lois today. She sent me a picture of a pier at Myrtle Beach where they have been on vacation. I saw a story about Hank Aaron getting close to Babe Ruth's home run record. He may beat him in numbers but the Babe made baseball what it is today.

July 24, 1973

Neelie came by today after I got back from the cemetery, but she didn't feel like working. She did feel like talking. She told me that Pete Morris had been arrested for stealing cows from old man John Ed Ray, who, like me, lives alone. I guess it was the same cows I saw Pete running across the old Vandiver place. I hope they put him on the chain gang. If the sheriff calls me to testify, I will. Anybody who would steal cows is no good and de-serves what the law gives him. Neelie said Arlie got scared and has stopped hanging around them Morris boys. Maybe it'll save him a jail term. I drove my truck out to examine the apple trees. It looks like a good crop, but I don't know if I'll dry out as many as I did last year. There's still a lot left. One of the things Cora cooked best was fried apple pies. Our girls try, but they don't do it the way she did. I got the light bill today ($12.15). Rates keep going up. Maybe I won't watch as much TV.

FOURTEEN

He began planning the trip before he opened the envelope containing the invitation. It was a subconscious act triggered by a quick vision coated on the translucent scrim of his imagination— being again among the people he had liked.

He knew what was in the envelope because of the name on the return address: Madison A&M Reunion Committee.

Sixty years, he thought, as he cut the seam of the envelope with his knife. Nineteen thirteen to nineteen seventy-three. Sixty years.

Dear Classmate:

Time marches on.

This is to remind you that the classes of Madison A&M from 1910 through 1915 are invited to gather at Morgan County High School (site of Madison A&M) on September 23, 1973, at 12 noon, to celebrate a reunion of special friends.

A luncheon is being planned, followed by an afternoon tour of our beloved and beautiful city. For those who want to visit and reminisce, we're also planning a dinner and will help with making arrangements to stay overnight.

Please make your plans to join us on this occasion. The years have given us all something to remember and to share. Your reunion committee looks forward to seeing you.

Sincerely,
Martha Dunaway Kerr ('15)
Chairlady

There was a registration card to be filled out and returned with a check for twenty dollars to cover the cost of the luncheon and the tour bus.

Cora had wanted to go to the reunion. On the day she died, the day the first invitation arrived, she had said she wanted to go. He remembered the eagerness of her voice.

He took his pen and put his name on the card and wrote a check for twenty dollars and slipped it inside the return envelope.

What if I'm the only one to show up? he wondered. God knows, we're all old as the hills. Most must be dead by now, scattered about in cemeteries like used-up utensils dumped in landfills. Maybe no one would return, except him, and it would be the last of the reunions. Maybe he would sit down with Martha Dunaway Kerr and the two of them would silently eat lunch in the empty lunchroom of Morgan County High School.

He chuckled suddenly at the image: two old people gnawing away on tasteless food, not knowing what to say, wishing before the Heavenly Father God Almighty that they were somewhere else. He could see curled crepe paper streamers thumbtacked to walls and balloons bobbing limply on tie-strings. And the banner — yes, there would be a banner — welcoming the alumni. He would sit in the center of that circus with Martha Dunaway Kerr and wonder what he should be saying to her.

He turned on his radio to listen to the noon news and the Obituary Column of the Air, but he did not hear the deep and solemn voice of the announcer. He thought of Martha Dunaway Kerr. She had been a feisty girl, he remembered, quick to laugh and quick for temper — a personality suited to her scrubbed Irish face and her reddish-blond hair. She did not live on the campus, but in one of the elegant homes of Madison, and she seemed to wear that elegance around her shoulders like an expensive shawl. The boys whispered about her — reverently, in awe. She was too fine for them, they believed. Too fine. None of them had the nerve to call for her at her home. None of them knew how to behave in such a refined environment.

He reread the invitation with Martha Dunaway Kerr's signature. There was still surety in the light, cursive sweep of her hand. It did not crawl and tremble in the making of letters, as his did, and he knew her voice would be the same — light, lilting, rushing to the next word and the next, her voice as cursive as her signature. But he wondered also if she would find him appropriate company for a conversation. She had married well, had moved comfortably in a cultured society, had become a figure of respect. He would be as tongue-tied at eighty in the company of Martha Dunaway Kerr as he had been at twenty-three.

The sorrowful organ music of the Obituary Column of the Air played from his radio. There were no announcements. No one had died.

He put the invitation from the Madison A&M Reunion Committee in his journal, where it would be safe from the prying, curious eyes of his prying, curious children. He did not want his children to know he would attend the reunion. He wanted to go alone, with dignity. He did not want to be transported by his daughters or sons, like fragile baggage.

"Just me and you," he said to White Dog, who lay beside his chair. "Just me and you."

At night, he wrote in his journal:

> Received a reminder to attend the Madison A&M reunion in today's mail. It's been many years since I was in Madison and I suppose it has changed, like everything else. I first went there as a 16-year-old boy on his own. I did not have a penny on me the day I arrived, but I went to the office and told them I was willing to work. They gave me a job on the farm. My years in Madison were the best of my life. It is where I met my wife and where we got married. The last time I went to Madison was with Cora, my wife. We visited with some old friends and had one of the best days of our later life together. Cora always loved the houses in Madison, some of the finest in the south. She always wanted to live in one, but we could never afford such luxury. We had to be content with our children being our luxury and they have been better than any house could be. I plan to go to the reunion. I will go alone, with my white dog to keep me company. I know my family would not let me do this if they knew about it, but I will not tell them. It has been a cool day for August and I have rested most of the time. Hoyt called and asked me if I wanted to go fishing with him tomorrow. He said Alma

*would spend the day with Kate and Carrie and then cook
supper for us. I told him I would. Maybe we'll catch some
catfish. It's been a long time since I had any and I like them.*

Of course, Hoyt told him. He would bring his tow hitch
down on Saturday and take away the truck and give it an engine
overhaul.

"Brakes, too," he said to Hoyt.

"All right, brakes, too."

"Better check it all out. Make sure the lights work and
windshield wipers."

"Why you want all this done?" Hoyt asked.

"One of these days the sheriff may stop me," he said. "Want
the truck working right, if he does."

"Might cost a good bit of money," advised Hoyt. "You'll be
needing some new parts."

"Just keep up with it. I'll give you a check."

Hoyt took another catfish from the serving platter and studied
his father-in-law suspiciously. In the years he had been married to
Alma, he had never known his father-in-law to give permission to
spend money without an accounting for every penny. There was
a family story that he had once discovered an over-charge from
the community store and had engaged the store owner in a stern
argument. Since that experience, he had always checked charges
against payment.

"Now, Daddy, Hoyt won't charge for anything but the
parts," Alma said soothingly. She poured more tea into his glass.
"But that might be more than you'd care to spend. Things like that
cost a lot these days."

He nodded an understanding. "Got to have my truck running right. Might break down in the field someday, and I'd have
to hobble home."

"Just so you know it might cost more than you think," Alma
said. She threw a puzzled question to Hoyt with her eyes.

"Maybe I can find some good used parts," Hoyt suggested.
"Won't be as much."

"Whatever you think," he said. "I trust you." He watched the
reluctant agreement in Hoyt's face, but he had been truthful: he
did trust his son-in-law. Hoyt was an honest man, a hard worker,

a good provider for his oldest daughter. And Hoyt had a way with engines. He could listen to a motor and point his finger toward a trouble spot, like a divining rod bending to water. He knew a sticking valve from a clogged carburetor, and he could take his tools and disappear beneath the raised, yawning hood of a car and bang about expertly.

"I'll get it Saturday, then," Hoyt said.

As they drove to their home, after Alma had washed and put away the supper dishes, Hoyt said, "Wonder what he's doing, wanting that old truck fixed up?"

"You've got me," Alma admitted. "Maybe he just wants it running right."

"Best thing he could do would be to take a forty-five and put a hole in its radiator. Just finish it off. God knows, it needs everything but a new front bumper, and that ain't in great shape, itself."

"He's acting funny, all right."

"Not like him to spend money without asking about every penny. That's what's got me."

"Me, too," Alma said. "But he wants it done, so we need to do it."

"That's done," he said to White Dog as he watched Hoyt's car crest Cemetery Hill in a swirl of sunset dust a half-mile away. He smiled proudly. "Poor old Hoyt. He thinks I've lost my mind." He stood leaning on his walker, his arms holding his weight. The heavy evening air was thick with the odor of grass and dust and flowering bushes. He inhaled slowly, deliberately, letting the perfumes seep into his senses. Other people did not like August because it seemed always hot and still, but August was one of his favorite times. In August, the seams of the earth cracked with a groundcover of growing, like a full, ripe flower spreading itself to the sun's heat, and the fragrance of the earth sweetened the air. He opened his mouth and let the air slide across his tongue, and he could taste its honey.

He did not watch television. He took a state map from his roll-top desk and spread it across the kitchen table and studied it carefully. The faint, squiggling lines of the map made his eyes burn and reminded him that he wanted a magnifying glass. It would be best to go the backroads, he reasoned. On the backroads, he could be any farmer going about business and no one would wonder about his old truck. Old farmers and old trucks were not uncommon. He took a yellow crayon left at his home by one of his grandchildren and marked the route.

The first time he went to Madison, a boyhood friend — Asa Cobb — had convinced him that it was the place for going to school. "You get out of there and they give you a hundred acres somewhere and it belongs to you," Asa had said. "All you got to do is farm it." The imagined land (it was only that; there were no gifts of property) had enticed him, and he had agreed to go on the train to Madison with Asa. On the day they were to leave, Asa had decided not to go. "Too far from home," was his excuse. "Well, I'm going," he had said to Asa. "Nothing around here for me." And that had been true. His parents were dead. He lived with an older brother's family. His older brother seemed always annoyed by him. He had taken the train to Madison and walked to the school and announced to the administrator, "I'm willing to work." The administrator had studied him through small, severe eyes. "There's work to be done," the administrator had said.

Sixty-five years since that train ride, he thought. Sixty-five years. He could still remember being frightened. "We'll take our time," he said to White Dog. "Might take all day, but it won't matter." He thought about the announced hour of the reunion. "Guess we better go the day before," he mumbled. "Start off early. Give us plenty of time. Used to be a hotel in town, if I remember it right. You can stay in the truck." He patted the dog on her head and laughed playfully. "Keep people from stealing it," he added.

FIFTEEN

On the Monday after Hoyt pulled his truck away to repair it, he asked Kate to drive him to the bank in town. She called Carrie.

"He asked you?" Carrie said. "He didn't tell you?"

"No. He asked. Polite-like," replied Kate. "He sounded, well, talkative. I haven't heard him sound like that in a long time, not since that time Neelie came over and he made out that we were still starving him."

"Maybe he's feeling better," suggested Carrie.

"Maybe. You know about his truck?"

"Holman told me. Said he wanted Hoyt to overhaul it. Do anything that it needed."

"Does that sound like him?" Kate said.

"Daddy? Our daddy? Lord, no. Holman said Hoyt was scared to death of spending too much."

"Sometimes old people get that way," Kate said. "I read about it in *Reader's Digest,* I think it was. They go hog-wild with money, spending it fast as they can. Has something to do with losing all sense of value. That article said they always begin to act childlike when they start spending. Said they didn't know the difference between a dime and a dollar."

"He said he wants you to take him to the bank?" Carrie asked skeptically.

"Oh, Lord, that's right."

"See if you can find out why," suggested Carrie.

"How am I supposed to do that?"

"Go in with him. Stay right beside him."

"Carrie, I may be dumb, but I'm not stupid. And I'm not crazy. He wouldn't even let Mama know what he did in a bank.

Made her wait in the car."

"Well, talk to him."

"I'll try," Kate said fretfully.

Kate knew he was in a spirited mood. He had bathed and shaved and had dressed in a colorful mismatching of brown suit and green shirt and blue tie. He smelled of talc and Mennen Skin Bracer. A white shred of toilet tissue covered a razor nick on his chin.

"You sure look, ah, all dressed up, Daddy," Kate told him as she helped him into her car.

"Like to put on my suit when I'm going to the bank," he said casually. "Want them to know I'm in for business."

"You got any special business you're doing, Daddy?"

"Nothing special," he said. "Just like to go in once in a while to let them know I'm still out here."

"Daddy, you ever wear those white shirts Noah and I gave you?"

"Don't like white," he said. "Shows dirt too easy. Gave them to James."

"Oh," Kate sighed. It was not the first time he had given away one of her gifts. He believed that a gift given was a gift gone and he could do with it as he pleased.

"Don't want to be buried in a white shirt, Kate. You keep that in mind. Just bury me in what I've got on. I like this shirt."

"It's a little frayed at the collar, Daddy."

"Won't many people be seeing it when they close the lid," he said. "Let's go. Bank's open already."

She watched him in quick, eye-darting glances as she drove to town. A pleasant smile was carved into his face. His eyes seemed bright and expectant.

"Great God," he exclaimed. "There goes my dog. She's following us, out there in the field." He pulled at Kate's arm and pointed to the field beside the car. White Dog rose and soared and fell and rose and soared again in powerful, graceful leaps. "Looks like a deer, don't she? Never saw a dog that fast. Guess maybe she's got some greyhound in her."

"Noah thinks so," Kate said. "Greyhound and German shepherd."

"She'll go up to the cemetery and wait there. We can drive by when I finish at the bank, and you'll see."

"If you want to," Kate said. Then: "Everything's all right at the bank, I hope."

"You already asked about that. Everything's fine. Just want to check my balance."

"You don't need any money, do you, Daddy?"

"I always need money, Kate, if you got some you're giving away."

Kate forced a laugh. "That's me, Daddy. Got money to burn."

"About all it's good for, anyhow," he said innocently. "The more you make, the more you spend. Might as well not have any."

Kate turned her face from the road to look at him. The magazine article had mentioned an attitude of disregard; money meant no more than paper. Old people afflicted with unreasonable spending habits had even tried to pay bills with wads of notebook paper.

"Daddy, I thought I might stop in at the store and buy some of those peppermint sticks you like," Kate said carefully. "How much do you think I ought to pay for them?"

He looked at her curiously. "What they charge."

"Wonder how much that is?" Kate said. "It's been a long time since I bought any. But you're always buying them. How much did you pay last time?"

"Good God, Kate. I don't remember. Might of been a penny a piece, or it might have been a nickel."

The magazine also said that afflicted people could not remember prices. "You think they could be a dollar a piece?" Kate asked.

He furrowed his brow and stared at her. He thought: She gets crazier by the day. God knows, it's sad, watching her get crazier. "A dollar?" he said. "Could be. Don't think they cost that much, though. But you want some, we'll stop by the store and get them."

It's true, Kate thought. He's afflicted. She could feel the weight of sadness in her face. She wanted to cry.

He took six hundred dollars from the bank and insisted Kate drive him to the store, where he purchased a jar of soft peppermint sticks and gave them to Kate. "Go ahead and eat one if you want it," he said gently. "Maybe I'll eat one with you."

"How much did they cost?" asked Kate.

"Not much," he said.

"Well, Daddy, they could have cheated you."

"Don't think so. They gave me money back."

"Did you count it?"

"Kate, what's the matter with you? No, I didn't count it. They counted it when they put it in my hand. Like they always do."

"I always count my change," Kate said, fighting tears.

He looked at her curiously. "That's good," he said in a kind voice.

When she returned home Kate called Carrie. "I was right," she said mournfully. "It was just like that magazine article said. He's got no idea what money's for anymore."

"What happened?"

"He said he'd just as soon burn money as spend it."

"What?"

"He didn't even know the cost of candy."

"Are you sure?" Carrie asked.

"Dead sure. We'd better call the others."

"Somebody's going to have to take over his affairs," Carrie suggested.

"Well, it won't be me," Kate replied tearfully. "It'd tear my heart out."

"Don't start crying, Kate. If you do, I will, too."

"I — I can't — can't help it."

"Don't, Kate."

The two sisters wept painfully into their telephones.

While his daughters spilled their tears, he wrote in his journal:

> I got my money for the reunion today, though I won't need it for a few weeks. Kate took me to town to get it, since I don't have my truck. I don't think Kate is well. She talked funny all day. If she keeps it up, I'll speak to Noah about her. I feel better than I have in a long time. My hip only hurts if I put too much weight on it and the new pills I've been taking help me sleep better than the old ones. Cora used to worry about me taking pills, but if they

help the pain I'll keep taking them. White Dog had a good time chasing Kate's car today. When we went by the cemetery she was there, waiting for me. I couldn't get her to ride in the car, though. I miss having my old truck around. Maybe Hoyt will have the work on it finished this week.

SIXTEEN

His reunion money was in a sock in the bottom drawer of his desk. He took it out often to assure himself that it was still there and had not been stolen while he slept in his unlocked house. He had never kept so much cash money with him, and he wondered why he had withdrawn six hundred dollars. Trying to be someone he wasn't, he guessed. He would need less than a hundred, by his calculations. Gas for his truck and lodging for two days and some food. It would be best to put five hundred back in the bank. Or maybe he would take one hundred and fifty on his trip. Maybe he would want to leave a donation for the reunion fund, though he doubted that he would ever again attend a reunion. Not at his age. Traveling great distances was tiring. Still, having one hundred and fifty dollars was not unreasonable for such a trip as he had planned. If his truck broke down, he would have enough money for its repair.

But his truck ran like a new machine. Hoyt had kept it almost two weeks, and the motor now purred with a quiet ticking, like a tightly wound pocket watch. With his failing hearing, he was not sure if the motor was running. In an odd way, he missed the clattering noise of loose metal beating against loose metal.

"You have to change gears when it's time to," warned Hoyt. "You don't, and it'll tear up again."

"All right," he said.

"I even got the windshield wipers working," Hoyt added proudly. "And the horn blows."

"Good Lord," he exclaimed softly. "Didn't know it had one."

Hoyt reached inside the cab of the truck and touched the horn cap in the center of the steering wheel. The horn squawked.

"I swear," he said in astonishment.

"You change gears when it's time to and keep the oil changed in it, it ought to run you two or three years before you need to do anything else," predicted Hoyt.

"When I die, I'm going to will you this old truck," he told Hoyt.

"Mr. Sam, that old truck'll be gone a long time before you."

"I doubt that," he said philosophically. "I got no more gears to change. It has."

He would take one hundred and fifty dollars to his reunion, he decided. Martha Dunaway Kerr would not feel pity for him if he demonstrated that he had money. And maybe he would buy a trinket for Kate and Carrie. If he returned with something for them, they would be distracted and not as harsh with him for not telling about the trip. They would probably cry, he thought. Lord, they were always crying about something.

He had his money and his map and his truck. He had his alibi about visiting Neal Lewis ready to tell. He had his suit and two shirts and two ties clean and pressed and hanging in his closet. He had a big sock for his razor and lather and Mennen Skin Bracer and pills.

There was nothing else he needed, but there was one thing he would carry with him: her picture. He had taken the picture in 1916 with Marshall Harris's borrowed camera when they were together at Madison. Marshall was in the picture with her, clowning. Marshall had his arm draped teasingly over her shoulder, and there was a foolish smile in Marshall's face. She, too, was smiling, but the smile had the girlish, blushed look of pleasant embarrassment. The central building of the campus was in the background of the picture, but it no longer existed. The buildings of Madison A&M had been bulldozed away, and Morgan County High School had been erected in its place. Brick columns at the entrances leading from the road onto the campus were the only reminders of Madison A&M. The columns had been established by graduating classes and on each there was a plaque containing names of the graduates. On his last visit to Madison — he did not remember the year, but he was with Cora — he had walked among the columns and read the names and it struck him that the columns were like leavings of an ancient civilization, with silent, guesswork histories set in curious markings.

Cora's picture — Cora's and Marshall's picture — was the only photograph he had ever privately kept. None of his children had seen it. It had always been in his book of records and his book of records had always been in his desk. When he did remove it and look at it — as he was now doing — it would call him to that exact, camera-click moment, a daybright spring afternoon ending the May Festival. All day they were together, with Marshall tagging after them, babbling his great, funny lies.

He touched the tiny image of her picture-face with his finger. She was beautiful.

He wanted to have the picture with him for the reunion. He would show it to Martha Dunaway Kerr.

On the afternoon of September 21, he drove his truck to the service station on Highway 29 and had the attendant fill its tank with gasoline. He also had the oil level checked. "Looks fine, Mr. Peek," the attendant said. "Looks like you had some work done on the motor. Want me to check the water and tires?"

"Look over what needs to be looked at," he said. "I'm taking a little trip tomorrow."

"Don't be going too far," the attendant said. "Old truck like this liable to break down, no matter what's been done to it."

"It'll get me there," he said confidently.

He had supper with Kate and Noah and told them he would be driving to Hartwell the next morning to spend one or two days with Neal Lewis.

"Neal's been after me to come over since his wife died," he said. "Wants me to look at some of his trees."

"You sure that's all he's got in mind, Mr. Sam?" Noah said playfully. "The two of you not planning to drive over to Anderson to one of them girl shows, are you?"

"Don't know," he replied casually. "Neal said he had a couple of friends he wanted me to meet. Maybe that's what he was talking about."

"Daddy," Kate exclaimed. "You ought to be ashamed of yourself."

"Leave your daddy alone," Noah said. "A man needs to get out once in a while. Maybe I'll go with him."

"Well, maybe you ought to. Maybe you ought to drive him over," Kate said.

"Going in my truck," he replied firmly.

"Daddy, you ought not be out on the highway in that old thing."

"Hoyt's got it running good," he argued. "It'll get me there."

"You don't even have a license, Daddy."

"Don't expect to need one," he said.

Noah did not want to hear an argument. He knew that Kate would not sleep from worry. "He'll be all right. I drove the truck the other day. It's in good shape." He looked at his father-in-law. "Only thing you've got to do is learn how to shift gears. You keep starting off in third gear, you'll strip everything in that gear box."

His father-in-law nodded absently.

The entry in his journal of September 21 read:

Everything ready for my trip to Madison. I put an old quilt in the cab of my truck for White Dog. Washed out two gallon milk jars for water that I will carry with me in case the radiator boils over. I'll cook some extra biscuits for White Dog to eat and make some sandwiches for myself. No need of spending more money that I have to. I'll also carry some Pepsi-Colas, which I like and can drink when they're warm. I don't like not telling my children what I'm doing, but I know how they would act. It was a cool day for this time of year, almost cold. The weather report said we may set records. I thought we already had. Don't ever remember it being this cold this early. I hope it warms up a little by tomorrow. I read a funny story in the paper today about Billy Jean King beating Bobby Riggs in a tennis match. The old fool ought to have known better than play a young woman, but I guess he's laughing, or maybe limping, all the way to the bank.

SEVENTEEN

It was still dark when he packed his suitcase — Cora's suitcase; he had never owned one — and clumsily balancing it across the top braces of his walker, carried it to his truck. It was cool outside, almost winter-cold, but he was eager to be away on his journey.

He cooked and ate his breakfast — grits and sausage and biscuits — and he fed White Dog from the leftovers of his plate. He then made his sandwiches and packed them with the extra biscuits for White Dog in a paper sack from Pennywise, and he filled his plastic water jars and carried them to his truck and placed them in the floorboard of the passenger's seat.

He made one last trip into his house — for his road map and for his journal and for Cora's picture, which he had left in his book of records. He wondered if Martha Dunaway Kerr would remember Cora or Marshall Harris, or himself.

"Come on," he said to White Dog, holding open the door of his truck. "Jump up in there. We're going on a trip." The dog looked quizzically at him, then sprang lightly into the cab of the truck and curled in the passenger's seat. A pale, morning spray of soft pink fanned across the black gum and poplar trees of the swamp. A mockingbird squawked absurdly loud in a pecan tree. "Got a long way to go," he said to White Dog as he pulled himself into the cab of the truck. He looked toward the houses of his two daughters. There were no lights on. At least he would be away, up the road, before they realized that he had left so early.

He touched the starter pedal with his foot, and the motor of the truck spit quietly and began to run easily. He pulled on the headlight switch and pushed in the clutch and eased the gear down and released the clutch. The truck jerked and sputtered and rolled laboriously forward. He wondered what gear the truck was in. Not the right one. But he was going forward and that was good enough. White Dog sat up and looked over the rim of the window. "Hold on, girl," he said merrily. "We're going to meet Martha Dunaway Kerr."

Carrie said into the telephone to Kate, "You hear the truck start up?"

"Noah did. I was still asleep. Noah said he left sometime around sunup."

"Still pitch-dark," Carrie said. "It woke me up. I looked out the window. Couldn't see a thing. Couldn't see your hand up at your nose, it was so dark."

"Maybe he just couldn't sleep and decided he'd get started early. Maybe he's going up by the cemetery first."

"Looks like he'd call one of us before he left like that," complained Carrie.

"You'd think so," agreed Kate. "But you know Daddy. Does whatever he wants to. I swear, sometimes I think he does things like that on purpose, just to aggravate us, like Noah says. Like he's always doing when Neelie's around."

"Sometimes I think the same thing," Carrie said. "How long did he said he'd be gone?"

"A couple of days, maybe. But he won't. He likes his own bed. He'll be back before this afternoon, if I know him."

"Has Daddy ever spent the night off with anybody that wadn't in the family?" asked Carrie.

"Not that I know of."

"Seems strange that he'd do that now. Don't you think it seems strange?"

"I don't know. You think it does?"

"He's been acting funny for a long time now."

"Don't start that again, Carrie. I didn't sleep for two days the last time you got started on Daddy acting like a child."

"Me?" Carrie said in astonishment. "I didn't bring that up. You did. Said you'd read something about it in *Reader's Digest*."

"Well, maybe I read the story, but you were the one who

wanted me to follow Daddy in the bank to see if he knew what he was doing."

"My Lord, Kate, don't go making a mountain out of a molehill. I just said it seemed funny to me that he'd go off and start spending the night with people that's not in the family. That's something one of my boys would do, not a grown man."

"There you go again, Carrie."

"What?"

"You said it was something a child would do."

"I said it was something one of my boys would do."

"It's the same thing."

"Kate, it's too early to argue. I haven't had my coffee yet. Did he say he'd call when he got there?"

"He didn't say he would. Maybe we ought to call over there and see if he got there all right."

"You got the number?" asked Carrie.

Kate sighed wearily into the phone. "He said he'd give it to me, but he didn't."

"You know the name of the man he's going to see?"

"Lewis," answered Kate. "Somebody Lewis."

"That's a big help," Carrie said bluntly. "Does Noah know?"

"I don't think so. Anyhow, he went in early today. I don't know why Daddy didn't leave me the number. He said he would."

"Well, let's just wait. If we don't hear from him by this afternoon, we can start trying to find him."

"The man's wife died not long ago," Kate said.

"What man's wife?" Carrie asked.

"The man he was going to see," Kate said. "We can call the radio station and get the obituary. It'll have his name."

"I guess so. If you hear anything let me know."

"Same with you," Kate said. Then: "I'll bet he knows right now how much he's got us worried. I'll bet he's having a big laugh over making us worry so much."

He was hopelessly lost, and he did not understand why. He had followed the crayon-coated line of his map — or believed he had — and still he did not see a road sign with the name of Madison on it.

It was late afternoon and the sun was in his eyes, blinding him, as he drove in sputtering slowness along the narrow dirt road that, on his map, should have been a paved highway. Maybe the map makers had made a mistake, he thought. It could be. People were always making such mistakes. He'd read about them often enough in magazines and newspapers, but if it was a mistake, somebody should have put up a sign saying the dirt road was a dirt road instead of a paved highway. "People don't much care anymore," he said to White Dog.

The man at the service station where he had stopped for gasoline and a check of his radiator should have said something to him about the road. Hadn't he told the man where he was going?

"Madison, huh?" the man had said. "You sure this old truck's gonna make it?"

"It'll make it. Looks bad, but it runs good."

"Hope you're right," the man had said pleasantly. "It's a long way off. Does the heater work on this thing?"

"Well, I don't know. Never tried it. It's warm enough inside. But the motor runs. It'll make it," he had repeated.

He pulled the truck to the side of the road, beneath the shade of an oak, and opened the door and White Dog leaped outside. "Go on and run around some," he said. "I guess you tired of being jerked around." He watched the dog slip cautiously into the brush by the roadside, then he said aloud as though calling to the dog, "I know we're going slow, but seems to me we should of been there a long time ago."

He took one of his Pepsi-Colas and opened it and drank from it. It was warm and sweet. Maybe it'd be best to rest a while, he decided. Let the sun go down some more, so it won't be in my eyes. Maybe look at the map again. God only knows what could have happened. Old eyes. Maybe they read the map wrong. Maybe they missed a turn-off.

He could not remember ever going to Madison on the route he had taken. And even before there were good roads and automobiles that could cover the distance with some speed, it had never taken so long to make the trip. God Almighty, he thought, it's only a hundred miles or a little more. Should of been there by lunchtime, even with stopping to rest. If I was younger and had two good legs, I could of walked it faster. Straight as the crow flies, I could of done it.

It had gone well enough early in the day. Being out at sunrise, there were few cars or trucks on the road and he had driven slowly enough to study his route, but somewhere near Athens, he seemed to be traveling southwest (by the pitch of the sun, at least) and he had been uncertain for hours.

There had been an occasional angry hornblast at him for his creeping pace, but he had ignored the impatience. People drove too fast for their own good. Little wonder there were so many accidents and so many killed. No reason to be in such a hurry.

He thought of a truck that had passed him earlier. It, too, was old — older than his own truck, he judged. The truck had eased up beside him, shuddering with great noise, and he had looked into the cab. The driver was also old — as old as he, perhaps older — and he held the steering wheel with a death grip. He remembered thinking, Good God, we must be a sight. Both of us ought to be in wheelchairs and both of us out on the road, like we're on a race-track for turtles. He had lifted his foot off the gas pedal, and the other truck had gradually moved around him.

Maybe I should have picked up the boy hitchhiking on the side of the road, he thought. Maybe the boy could have told me which roads to follow to find Madison.

He had wanted to stop for the boy, had lifted his foot from the accelator to touch the brake, but he had not stopped. The boy looked tired, standing with his suitcase in one hand, the other hand up, curled in a fist, thumb out in the hitchhiker's begging sign language. When he passed the boy, driving slow, he could see the boy's eyes watching him hopefully, a small, crooked smile on his lips. And he had thought of his own son standing on a roadside, taking the ride that would deliver him to his death. His own son would have had hopeful eyes and a small, crooked smile.

He leaned heavily against the seat of his truck and closed his eyes and fought to keep from crying. The presence of his son, of Thomas, entered him through the opened mouth of his deep, tremulous breathing and filled him with ancient regret. He had buried his son; he had never buried the hurt. He saw again the boy on the road, asking silently for a ride. His own son had died in a truck. He could not risk the life of another man's son and he could not have the specter of his own son riding with him in the body of someone else.

He rolled down the window of his truck and forced himself to breathe slowly, evenly. The day had remained cool in the way that autumn-becoming-winter is cool, and as he sat in his truck on the roadside waiting for his dog to run in the fields, he felt a sudden chill shimmering on his arms. He knew the chill was only partly because of the autumn cool. He was alone. He was alone on a road he did not know, and it was late in the afternoon.

He called to White Dog from his truck, "Come on, girl. We got to go. Come on." The dog heard him and raced back to the truck and jumped into the cab through the opened door. "We got to find out where we are," he said to the dog. "Looks like we lost." He laughed nervously. "Old man and a dog. Lost."

EIGHTEEN

It was an argument that Noah and Holman would regret. They said to Kate and Carrie, "Leave your daddy alone. He's a grown man. If he wants to call to let you know how he is, he will, but that's up to him. He knows how to take care of himself. Besides, if anything had happened to him on the way over to Hartwell, we'd know it by now. Somebody would've called us. Good Lord, everybody in the county knows who he is. He's probably got trees in every yard in a forty-mile radius."

"Well, I'm calling," Kate said defiantly. "I don't care what either one of you say."

"I'm with Kate," Carrie declared.

It was almost six o'clock in the afternoon and the sisters and their husbands were sitting in the kitchen of Kate and Noah's home. For two hours, Kate and Carrie had sat at the table, drinking coffee, fretting, waiting by the telephone.

"When he blesses you out, don't blame me," Noah said. "No wonder he's always aggravating the two of you. You got to give him some peace."

"Noah's right," Holman said firmly. "Good God, once in a while a man's just got to get off by himself, without everybody hanging over him like a cloud."

"Shut up, Holman," Carrie snapped.

Holman sighed and shrugged.

"Let 'em do it," Noah said. "They ain't going to be happy if they don't."

"Waste of time," Holman mumbled.

The telephone call to the radio station revealed that it was

Neal Lewis's wife who had died. The station's switchboard operator gave Kate the number for the Lewis residence.

"Sam Peek?" Neal Lewis said in his shouting telephone voice. "Ain't seen Sam since Hattie passed on. Who did you say you was?"

"It ain't like Mr. Sam to go off without letting somebody know where he is," Clete Walton said quietly to Noah and Holman. "It ain't like him. I've known that man all my life, ever since I was knee-high to a grasshopper." Clete was the county sheriff. He stood with Noah and Holman outside the house in the thick, dull light of early evening, smoking a cigarette. Inside, Kate and Carrie waited fearfully for the arrival of their sisters and brothers.

"Kate thinks he's been acting strange the last few weeks," Noah said.

"Carrie, too," agreed Holman.

"Well, old people get that way sometimes. Especially after they have somebody pass on and they left alone," Clete said. "My daddy got that way after my mama passed on. God knows, it ain't a good thing to watch happen."

"Maybe that old truck broke down," Holman said.

"I doubt it," Noah said. "It was in good shape, even if Mr. Sam don't know the first thing about changing gears. That's what he could of done. He could of ripped them out."

Clete drew deep from his cigarette and spewed the smoke through tight lips. "He ought not be driving that old truck off this farm. Don't know why y'all let him do it."

"I thought you knew him," Noah said firmly.

"I do," Clete replied.

"Then you know he ain't about to be told what he can and can't do. You ever tried to tell an old person what to do?"

"You got a point, Noah," admitted Clete. He stepped on his cigarette. "Well, I got every car in the department out, looking the roads between here and town. Told them to stop at all the creek bridges and take a close look. Sometimes old people get scared going over them narrow wood bridges. Old man Darby Pilgrim drove off the one down below his house last year and damned near drowned before they pulled him out."

"Good God, don't say nothing like that in front of them girls," warned Holman. "They'll go slap crazy."

"I won't," promised Clete. "I know how it is, boys. A woman gets worked up over her daddy. God knows, they do. I'd just as soon tell my woman I was fooling around with the neighbor lady as to tell her I think her daddy's crazy — which he is, by the way. Crazy as a damn loon. But I ain't about to say it to her. A woman gets worked up when it comes to her daddy."

"I just hope he's all right," Holman said softly. "I like that old man."

"Yeah," said Noah.

"It's going to be too dark to look much longer," Clete said.

He had not been frightened in years. Now he was.

He had driven frantically along dirt roads, trying to find a highway, using the sun for direction. But the sun had slipped below the lip of the horizon and he was tired from his day of driving and from the confusion of being lost. "Guess we better stop for the night," he said to the dog now nestled close to him, her face against his leg. "Guess we better find a place to stop."

He saw a deserted tenant farmhouse off the road, and he guided his truck over the eroded road and stopped beneath the canopy of an oak tree in the cluttered front yard. He opened the door of his truck and pulled himself out, taking his walker from the truck body. White Dog jumped from the truck and circled the yard, her head lowered suspiciously. She trotted back to him.

"See anything, girl?" he asked

The dog lifted her front feet to the top brace of the walker. He scratched her head playfully.

"Be dark in a few minutes," he said. "Guess you must be hungry."

He took biscuits from his food sack and fed White Dog, then poured water from one of his plastic milk jars into the palm of his hand and let the dog lap the water. He was not hungry, but he ate one of the biscuits and then took his pills for the pain that smoldered in his hip. He had been too long in the truck, too long sitting, and he knew he would suffer. "Won't sleep much to-night," he said to the dog.

And maybe he should not sleep, he thought. He knew of

deserted tenant houses where men gathered to gamble and to drink and sometimes there were fights and killings. An old man in an old truck would be easy takings for men who came out after dark for no-good reasons.

He was glad he had put the quilt for White Dog into the truck. The night quickly became cold, and he stretched across the cab seat with the quilt pulled over him. He had thought of going inside the house and making a fire in the fireplace, but he did not trust the rotted flooring that he saw through the opened door. He could break a leg falling through the floor, and even if he did not fall through, even if he got a fire started, the house could catch fire and if it did, it would burn in a flash and he, being slow-moving on his walker, would burn with it.

He would not sleep well. He would shiver beneath the quilt and ache from pain, and he would be afraid.

NINETEEN

Neelie was seated at the kitchen table, among the sons and daughters of Sam Peek, and she was saying again (in her way of saying it) that old men in old trucks should be watched over.

"Lord, Jesus, you babies got to take that old rattletrap away from him — if he be found alive. That old rattletrap liable to blow up on him out on the road. Maybe that's what it done. Blowed up. Blowed up when he was driving down the road. Blowed up and him in it. Old folks ought not be out driving. Neelie don't drive none. Never had no car. Never wanted none."

No one replied to Neelie. Replies encouraged outbursts.

"I been telling him, 'Mr. Sam, you keep out of that old truck.' What's he gon' do when it stop on him? He gon' walk? Babies, he can't hardly get about like it is. Breaks Neelie's heart watching him try to get about. Looks like he ain't gon' take another step, dragging that old leg along."

Carrie's eyes dampened at the image of her father, dragging his leg as he moved painfully along on his walker.

"Lord, Jesus," Neelie said again in a pronouncement.

It was past ten. Since she had arrived earlier — brought to the house by Holman after she had commanded a ride — Neelie had talked incessantly and the sons and daughters of Sam Peek were numb from the shrill, badgering voice, but for a reason they did not clearly understand, there was comfort in Neelie's presence and in Neelie's mournful soliloquies. For most of them, Neelie was their surrogate parent and it was a parent they needed.

Neelie had entered the house dramatically, struggling to walk under the burden of the sad news of Sam Peek's disappearance, wailing her despair. She had been assisted to the kitchen table by Carrie and Kate and immediately began her contention that Sam Peek was a changed man and that change was caused by the ghost dog.

"I seen ghost dogs," she asserted. "Them dogs don't bark. Don't never know where they be hiding. You be looking at a ghost dog and you blink your eyes and they gone. Ghost dogs always coming around when somebody passes on. Babies, your daddy's done changed on account of that ghost dog. Where that dog now? That dog ain't nowhere around. That dog with your daddy. That dog done took Mr. Sam off somewheres."

Kate, too, had wondered about the dog. Before the sheriff arrived, she had sent Noah to look for the dog, and Noah had returned to say the dog was missing.

"Maybe he took the dog with him," Noah had suggested. "Or maybe she ran off and he went looking for her."

Kate repeated what Noah had said.

"Could be," Sam, Jr. said. He had arrived thirty minutes earlier from Tennessee. The strain of the hurried drive was in his eyes.

"Ain't so," argued Neelie. "I seen ghost dogs. I seen one when I was a little girl. Black like the night, child. Big as a goat. Had them kind of eyes that was always shining like they was coals of fire out of a stove. Carried off a baby, that ghost dog did. Took it up in its mouth and dragged it off down in the woods and don't nobody never find that baby. My mama say it was a ghost dog mad at that baby's daddy for being mean. That dog with Mr. Sam, it a ghost dog."

"Neelie, don't say that," begged Carrie. "You're scaring me."

Neelie clucked her tongue and wagged her head seriously. "Ain't nothing to do but wait and see where Mr. Sam got off to," she said.

"But why'd he tell us he was going to see Neal Lewis, and Neal Lewis didn't know anything about it?" Kate asked.

"You ever see a ghost dog, babies, you better turn the other way and don't never look back on it," Neelie asserted. "Honey —" she was addressing Carrie "— why don't you pour Neelie a little bit more of that coffee, and while you up, call over to the sheriff and see what they doing."

"They're in bed, Neelie," Alma said wearily. "They said they'd start looking again in the morning."

"Lord, Jesus, poor old Mr. Sam. Hope them Morris boys ain't got him," Neelie muttered.

James lifted his head alertly. He said, "What do you mean, Neelie?"

Neelie waved a hand toward James. "Honey, your daddy saw one of them sorry boys with some cows they done stole from Mr. John Ed. He told the sheriff, and they put that sorry boy in the jail."

"When?" James asked. He was standing. The muscles in his face twitched.

"Oh, baby, that was back more'n a month now, maybe longer."

"They had his trial last week," Kate said. "He got four or five years, I think."

"Did the sheriff go over there to look?" James asked irritably.

No one knew. Paul said, "You'd think he would under the circumstances."

"Damn it," James muttered. He whirled and walked out of the kitchen. His brothers and sisters watched in bewilderment.

"What's he going to do?" whispered Carrie.

"I think we'd better go with him, Paul," Sam, Jr. said.

"I think you'd better try to stop him and call the sheriff," advised Alma. "You know how James is about Daddy. If he thinks that anybody's hurt him . . ." She did not finish the sentence.

"Oh, God," Kate moaned.

"James *is* the law, Alma," Lois said.

"Not here," Alma replied. She added, "Maybe I better call Hoyt. He's out with Noah and Holman. I think Hoyt knows that Morris man."

"Tell all of them to go," Kate begged.

"Wait a minute. Just wait," Sam, Jr. said firmly. "Let us handle this. If that's where James is going, we'll go with him. No need to send over a crowd."

His sisters were silent. It was a family of patriarchal order, and his sisters understood the right of their brother. He was the oldest living son. Such matters were his responsibility.

"Lord, Jesus," Neelie moaned desperately. "Them Morris boys is mean."

"It'll be all right," Sam, Jr. said. He looked at Carrie. "Maybe Holman can take Neelie home, since it's so late."

Carrie glanced quickly at Neelie. Neelie would leave when she wanted to leave. "I'll see," she replied meekly.

James was in his car, driving away, when Sam, Jr. and Paul stopped him and got into the car with him.

"What're you going to do?" asked Paul.

"Find out if they know anything about Daddy," James said.

"Shouldn't you call the sheriff? Let him go with you," Sam, Jr. suggested.

James looked coolly at his brother. He said, "I'll take care of it." Sam, Jr. had never seen James so angry. But it was not temper. It was anger triggered by fear. There was a scent of danger in the car.

"Just remember, you can't go accusing them without some proof," Paul advised from the back seat.

"Paul, I know what I'm doing," James replied. "This is my pulpit, not yours. You let me handle it."

The Morris house was isolated on a dirt road leading from the Goldmine ridge. The house was small and in disrepair. The yards were cluttered with trash and rusting parts of cars and farm equipment. A light was on in one of the rooms. James stopped the car in the front yard, with the light beams on the front door.

"You stay right here," James said to his brothers. It was not a request; it was an order.

"Keep your temper," Sam, Jr. said. He saw the pistol holstered to James' belt. He remembered being with James and Arlie one day at a small pond below their father's home when James had the pistol with him. Arlie had asked, "You hit anything with that little gun?" And James had slipped the pistol from its holster and aimed it at a can floating in the pond. "A little," James had replied. And then he had fired into the can in six rapid shots, with the can dancing over the surface of the water. Sam, Jr. remembered being in awe of his brother's skill.

"You going to take your gun with you?" Sam, Jr. asked.

James did not answer. He pushed on the horn of his car and

opened the door and got out and walked in front of the light beams. The light in the house snapped off.

"Herman Morris," James called in a loud voice, "I want to see you."

There was a moment of silence, and then, from the house, "Who's out there?"

"James Peek," James snapped.

"Well, boy, you better back off. You got a gun pointed right at you," the voice from the house growled.

"Sam," Paul whispered in the car.

"We'll make it worse if we get out," Sam, Jr. replied.

James took a step forward. He snapped his pistol free of its holster and held it in the air.

"You'd better be a damned good shot," he said calmly. "Because I am. Now come out here."

Again a pause. Then: "Who'd you say you was?"

"James Peek. Sam Peek's son. I'm a federal agent."

"What the hell you want with me?"

"I want to know if you've seen my father."

The light came on in the house, and the front door opened slowly. A thin man dressed in overalls and a faded work shirt stepped cautiously onto the porch. He held a rifle with a scope. He squinted his eyes at the light from the car beams.

"Well, boy, ain't no call to come up scaring a man's family," Herman Morris said bitterly. "No, I ain't seen your daddy. Why're you asking me?"

"He's missing. Maybe you got a reason to know about it."

Herman Morris stared at the pistol in James' hand. "Boy, I don't know what in hell's name you talking about. I ain't seen your daddy in a year or more. I heard tell he was laid up."

"Where're your boys?" James demanded.

"They ain't here."

"Where are they?"

"Two of them's working up in Virginia. The other's in jail, but I guess you know about that."

"How long they been in Virginia?"

"A week. Maybe more."

James relaxed his hand. He walked to the porch, near Herman Morris. He said quietly, "Mr. Morris, you take a good look at me.

There's nothing on the face of this earth I love more than that old man. If anybody ever put a finger on him, they'd know what I mean. You tell your boys that. You tell them to ask Arlie about me. Now I've got two preacher brothers sitting out there in the car and I expect they're scared to death right now, worrying about our souls. But they don't know you; I do. And I don't want them to. I want them to keep having faith. If you know anything about my daddy, you better tell me now."

James could see confusion in Herman Morris' face. He saw a man who was tired and old before his years to be old, and he felt a surge of pity for the man standing before him.

"I ain't seen him, boy," Herman Morris said softly. "Hope you find him, though. He's a good man. Give me some trees one time, and some grapevines. Any of my boys ever bothered him, they'd have me to answer to."

James slipped his pistol back into its holster. He knew Herman Morris was telling him the truth. The temper drained from him. He could feel his hand trembling.

"Sorry I upset you, Mr. Morris," he said. "Coming up like that. He's my daddy. And I don't know where he is."

Herman Morris nodded. He turned and went back into his house.

In the car, watching, Paul said to Sam, Jr., "I pray to God nobody's hurt Daddy. If they have, I pray somebody gets to them before James."

"I know," Sam, Jr. said. "But let's not say anything to him. Not now."

"Don't worry. I won't," Paul whispered.

"I don't think anybody's hurt him. I think he got lost. What I'm worried about is how cold it is tonight. The cold hurts his hip."

"I hope he had his pills," Paul said.

"He did. Alma said she checked. Said they were gone."

"And he's got the dog."

"Yes, he's got the dog."

His legs were cramped in the seat of the truck cab, and when he moved them spurts of pain stabbed through his hip, causing him to cry out softly. A wind blew briskly from the northwest, low to the ground, skimming over the field below the tenant farm-house and swirling around his truck. The wind seeped into the truck, into the quilt and the clothing covering him, and he could feel it clamping to his skin. He could not remember being so cold. He put his head against the cushion that he used to sit on when he drove and he tried to sleep. When he did — lightly, fitfully — he dreamed of Cora.

They were walking across a meadow toward a distant stand of pines and, near it, a wide stream that curled through the farm owned by Madison A&M. It was his favorite place on the farm, and he had promised to take her there. The day was bright, clear, green, with the sweet aroma of grasses and wildflowers swimming against their faces.

"Somebody might see us going down there," she said tentatively.

"Let them," he replied confidently. "See if I care."

"There's rules —"

"What're we doing?" he demanded. "We just walking. Nothing wrong with that."

"I just wonder what people would think, seeing us going off in the woods."

"Well, I don't care. I'm just showing you the farm, like I would anybody that wanted to see it. Everybody ought to see the farm."

"You could get fired," she cautioned.

He laughed. "They're not going to fire me. Be hard for them to find somebody else that'd do what they got me doing."

"If they do, don't say I didn't warn you."

"I won't."

They crossed the meadow and walked along the sandy rim of the pine tree stand until they could no longer see the buildings of the school, and then he stepped into the woods. She followed him hesitantly.

"Come on," he urged. "It's not as hot in here. Besides, it's like walking on a pillow."

He was right. The lush brown covering of fallen needles was a cushion for the step, and under the umbrella of towering limbs above them, the air was surprisingly cool.

"You like it here?" he asked.

"Yes," she said.

"First day I was at this school, I came down here," he told her. "There's a hickory tree down by the creek. I went down there and got a leaf off it and chewed on it, and I was all right."

She looked at him with a strange, questioning expression. "You ate a leaf?"

"Uh-huh. Sure did. Well, to tell the truth, I just bit it. I like trees. You take a bite out of a leaf, you know if it's good wood or not."

"How?"

He smiled shyly. "It's a secret."

"I don't believe you."

"It's true," he vowed. "But you got to like trees. I'd rather be with trees than most people I know. Someday I'm going to have me a tree nursery. That's what I'm going to do. Grow trees."

They strolled through the pines, talking. He knew he was bragging, like Marshall Harris bragged, but he enjoyed telling her about himself.

"Listen," he said.

"What?"

"The creek." She heard it. The gurgling of water near them.

"There's a lot of moss down near the creek. It's all over the place," he said. "Smells good."

She lifted her face and inhaled slowly. "Yes. It's musty."

"I like it," he said, smiling. "Sometimes I come down here just to smell it. Reminds me of when I was little and used to go fishing down on a creek near where my brother lived."

"Let's go see it," she said.

They sat on the creek bank, above an outcropping of granite that rippled like a gray muscle across the creek and into the opposite bank, and she leaned against his shoulder, silently watching the white spew of water spinning over the flat granite shoals.

"Like it?" he asked.

She nodded.

"Cora?"

"Yes."

"I want to marry you." He said the words easily, surprising himself.

134

She did not answer, but her head moved against his shoulder.

"How many children do you want?" he asked bravely.

"I don't know," she said.

"I want a lot. I want them all over the place."

"Why?"

"Just do. Always wanted a big family."

"Yes," she said.

"Yes, what?"

"Yes, I'll marry you."

In his dream, he saw her face that day. Her eyes were like light through translucent gemstones of hazel and brown. Her eyes were looking into him, asking questions.

"What's the matter?" he asked.

She blinked and a moist film covered the gemstones and he saw nothing but gladness. "Nothing," she answered softly.

He awoke with a shudder of pain. He could hear the wind whistling around the truck, and he could feel the cold biting into him. Beside him, curled in the floorboard of the truck, the white dog whimpered and rose and moved close to him, nudging her face against his chest. He looked at the dog, into the dog's eyes, and he saw Cora's eyes, the gemstones of hazel and brown. With a cry he pulled the dog to him and held to her.

TWENTY

The tapping above his head woke him, and in the wakening moment, in the murky semi-consciousness of that moment, he did not know where he was or what was happening around him. His body ached, and the pain in his hip caused him to swallow hard for breath. He was still cold. He heard the tapping again.

"Mister?"

The voice was loud, and the tapping on the window became a knocking. He caught the steering wheel and pulled himself up and looked through the window. The pain in his hip exploded in his brain and he felt faint.

"You all right, Mister?"

He bowed his head to fight the pain.

"Can you roll down the window, Mister?"

He sat, breathing in quick, shallow sips of air. Then his breathing eased, and he looked up at the man beside his truck. The man had the dried, lined face of a farm worker. He wore a bill cap with an insignia of a bulldozer. His denim jacket was buttoned tight against his throat.

"Can you roll down the window a little bit?" the man said again.

He turned the handle and rolled the window down halfway, and the man looked into the truck suspiciously.

"You look sick," the man said. "How'd you get out here?"

"Don't know," he admitted. "Got turned around. Got myself lost."

"My boy saw the truck up here earlier this morning. Said he looked in it. Said he thought they was a dead man in it. He come to get me." The man gestured with his head. "He's parked over there."

He looked in the direction the man gestured and saw a car. A young man, dressed like his father, stood behind the opened door of the car, as though shielding himself.

"You must be half-froze," the man said. "It got down close to frost last night."

He nodded. The cold and the pain from his hip had made him nauseous.

"Need to get out and stretch some?" the man asked.

"I guess," he said.

The man opened the door and held it.

He pulled himself to the edge of the door and placed his left foot on the running board of the truck. "Mind handing me that walker in the back?" he asked the man. "Can't get about without it."

"Yes sir," the man said. He took the walker from the bed of the truck and placed it on the ground and held it. "Take your time."

He stood with his weight on his good leg and with his hands pressed on the walker, his arms locked straight, and he tried to move his bad leg. He could feel blood pumping hard in his throat and arms.

"Need some help?" the man asked.

He shook his head. "Been cramped up all night. It'll take a minute."

"My mama had a bad hip," the man said. "She used one of them things. I know how it is."

He thought he heard his dog whimper behind him and he said, "If you step back a little bit, I'll get my dog out."

The man smiled quizzically. "What dog you talking about?"

He turned and looked back into the truck. White Dog was not there. "My dog was with me last night," he said firmly. He scanned the yard of the tenant farm house. "I must of let her out," he mumbled, but he did not remember.

"I'll have my boy look for her," the man said. "What's she look like?"

"White. Solid white," he said.

The man looked quickly at his son and nodded once. His son

looked away. "May be what my boy saw this morning," the man said. "Told me he was driving on the road when he saw something white jump up in the fields. Thought it was a deer at first."

"White Dog," he said. "My dog. Your boy won't find her. She's skittish. Won't have nothing to do with nobody but me. She was a stray that took up when I started giving her some scraps."

"Stray dogs is like that sometimes," the man said. Then: "My name's Howard Cook. I live down the road, about a mile from here. Used to live here, in this place, when I was little."

He extended his hand to Howard Cook. He said, "Sam Peek."

"Where you from, Mr. Peek?"

"Over in Hart County."

"You a long way from home," Howard Cook said. "What brings you over this way?"

"Going over to Madison," he said. "Started out yesterday morning, but I guess I missed a road somewhere."

"Guess you must have missed more'n one if you still on the way," Howard Cook said. "Why don't you let me drive you down to my house and get you some coffee and something to eat."

"Much obliged," he said, "but no need of that. You show me how to get back on the right road, and I'll stop off someplace."

"Nothing around here to stop at," Howard Cook said easily. "We kind of off the beaten path, and I'd feel a lot better about it if you'd let me drive you back down to my place. I do some preaching on Sunday at a little church not far from here. Preached about the Good Samaritan last week. Got to practice what I preach."

"I got two boys that preach," he said.

"Well, there, the Lord's got His hand in this," Howard Cook said. "I bet them boys has been praying for you, and the Lord's done delivered you to me." A smile eased into his farm-worker face. "I guess you'd want them boys of yours to be doing the same thing if they was in my place."

Howard Cook, weekday farmer and Sunday preacher, lived with his wife, Mildred, and his son, Kenneth, in a large, once-grand house. "She sags a little bit," Howard explained to Sam Peek, "but ever since I was a little boy I wanted to live in this house.

Used to be the prettiest place around, when Coy Mize and his folks owned it. They used to own about everything around here, but the children all left and when Coy and his wife died, they just sold everything off. When I got out of the Army I was able to get it for a fair price. Needs some work, but it beats that old house where you spent the night."

He was sitting at the kitchen table in Howard Cook's home, nibbling at the generous breakfast before him. He was hungry, but he could no longer swallow easily, and he now ate in small bites, softening the food until it was comfortable in his throat. He had taken his pills, and the pain in his hip had eased. He felt surprisingly alert with so little sleep from his night in the truck.

"You want some more coffee, Mr. Peek?" Mildred Cook asked.

He shook his head, swallowed, and said, "Got enough, thank you."

"You looking a lot better than you was a while ago," Howard said. "Got you some color in your face."

"Feel better than I did," he admitted. "Food's good, real good. Guess them sandwiches I had yesterday didn't do much for me."

"A person needs hot food," Mildred Cook declared cheerfully. "Don't know how a person gets by on nothing but sandwiches and that kind of stuff."

"What time you say you needed to be in Madison, Mr. Peek?" Howard asked.

"Before lunch," he said. "But I won't be eating much when I get there, not with all this food."

"Well, now, you'll have some time to get a little rest before you start out," Howard said. "You not that far away. Fifteen miles or so. We just out of Greensboro."

"I don't drive fast," he said.

"Don't need to," Howard replied. "Your truck's in pretty good shape from what I can tell, but it ain't ready for no race. Gears seem to be a little loose on it. Guess you better have that looked after when you get home."

He nodded and sipped from his coffee. He thought of Hoyt's warning. Hoyt would be annoyed to know the gears were loose.

"Tell you what," Howard continued, "I was planning to go over to Madison myself today. I can go on in this morning, and you can follow along." He looked at his wife and saw the bewildered question in her face. "Mildred was saying last night I ought to go on over this morning and get it over with."

"Yes," Mildred Cook said quickly, understanding her husband. "Never did like to put things off. If you got something to do, do it."

"Don't want to put you out more'n I have," he said.

"Now, Mr. Peek, would them boys of yours feel put out?" asked Howard.

After breakfast, he was led by Mildred Cook to a large, cushioned armchair with an ottoman and though he had protested mildly that he did not need rest, he was asleep within minutes.

In the kitchen, Howard sat at the table with a roadmap spread before him. "Best I can figure it," he said to his wife, "he was trying to dodge the main roads. He was talking about Comer and Lexington. Looks like he turned off at Bowman and went down to Comer and then over to Lexington, then maybe down toward Washington and on down to Sharon and over to Crawfordville, then back up twenty-two to where it runs into forty-four. Guess he must of took a left there, unless he got on one of them sideroads that cuts through. One thing for sure, he got lost out of Union Point. Had to."

"How'd he get so turned around?" his wife asked. She was washing the breakfast dishes.

Howard laughed quietly, gently. "He showed me his map. It must have come out of the Forties. Had him a line marked on it. Looked like it was crayon. Guess he don't see too good. Part of where he had marked was the Broad River, right down the middle of it. Thank the Lord he missed that turn."

Mildred Cook smiled. "He's a nice old man," she said. "You can tell. Looks like he's a little scared. You ought to call his folks."

Howard folded his map. "I was thinking about it," he admitted. "But I don't know. Don't like meddling in a man's life. Don't mind helping a man out, but they ain't no need to meddle."

"Maybe they're worried about him."

"He didn't let on they would be. Said they knew he was gon' be away for a couple of days."

"Why's he going to Madison?"

"Said he went to school there. Said they was a reunion."

"He say anything about his wife?"

"Didn't say and I didn't ask. I'd guess she was dead. All he said was he had a couple of boys who were preachers. Seemed more worried about his dog than he did anything else. Wadn't easy about leaving the old place, but he said she'd follow the truck. I didn't see nothing."

"She must be hiding out around the barn if she did," Mildred Cook said. "I haven't seen the first sign of a dog. You'd think our dogs would be barking their heads off if another dog was around."

Howard shook his head. "Don't know. Kenneth said he guessed what he saw might've been a dog. Said he never saw one that white." He chuckled. "Told me it scared him. Said he could feel something watching him driving down the road, and when he looked out the window, he saw something white. Said he almost drove in the gully."

"Well, I'm glad you're driving over to Madison so he can follow you. Didn't know what you were talking about at first." She was proud of her husband; it was in her voice.

"Don't guess he'd take to me driving him. It was one thing driving him over here, but taking him on over to Madison would be something else. Old people like than can be stubborn. Like your daddy was. No, I'd guess he'd want to get there on his own, since he struck out on his own. Having him follow me was the next best thing I could think of."

"He's sure sleeping sound," Mildred Cook said.

"Yeah. I can hear him snoring from in here," her husband replied.

"Be a pity to wake him."

"We can wait a little while. We'll leave about ten-thirty. Give him plenty of time. Let's get him up in time to wash his face and get dressed like he wants to."

"I thought I'd iron out that shirt he had in the truck," Mildred Cook said.

"He'll appreciate it. Think I'll go check out that old truck. See if it needs any oil or water."

"Wish you'd call and see if you can find his people," Mildred Cook said again.

"I'll think about it," her husband promised.

TWENTY-ONE

Clete Walton appeared at Sam Peek's home at nine o'clock. An aging deputy named George Detwilder was with him. The two men waited in the living room for Sam Peek's sons — Sam, Jr., Paul, James — and daughters — Alma, Lois, Kate, Carrie — to join them.

All except James quickly gathered.

"Maybe we got a little bit of a break," Clete announced.

"What?" Carrie asked anxiously.

"Spencer Fields — everybody here knows him, I guess — anyway, Spencer called me this morning, right before I was getting ready to leave home. Told me he'd seen Mr. Sam's truck going out over toward the Elberton road early yesterday morning. Said he wondered what Mr. Sam was doing, going out that way, but he didn't think nothing much about it. Spencer was coming in from working the night shift up at the mill and he didn't know nothing about Mr. Sam being gone, with him sleeping all day like he does. Said he heard about it up at the mill this morning, when he was getting off work."

"The Elberton road," Paul said, puzzled. "Why would he be going out that way?"

No one knew. There was no reason. He never drove to Elberton alone. He did not like driving among the huge trucks that transported slabs of granite from the quarries to the finishing sheds.

"Maybe he just got turned around," George Detwilder suggested somberly. "Thought he was going out over toward Hartwell and took off in the wrong direction. Old people do that sometimes."

"Well, they do at that," Clete said. "They's an old woman over in Bio — Harper's her name. She's always getting lost. Just gets out and starts to walking and goes anywhere her nose leads her. We had to find her a couple of times last year. Said she was out picking blackberries."

"She was barefoot, both times," George Detwilder added.

"She was," Clete said.

"I don't think Daddy's that forgetful," Sam, Jr. said. "As far as we know, he's still got his faculties." He looked at Alma, and she nodded confirmation. "What will you do, now?" he asked the sheriff. "Concentrate on the Elberton road area?"

Clete turned the sheriff's hat he held in his hands and absently wiped at the brim with his fingers. His face was furrowed in thought. Finally, he said, "That's what we're doing. I already got some cars over there, looking around, and I called the sheriff in Elbert and Franklin County. Told them to start looking around. They all know Mr. Sam."

"What about the State Patrol?" Paul asked.

"Did that, too," Clete replied. "Told them what the truck looked like. It ought to be easy enough to spot."

"If it didn't blow up, like Neelie said," Carrie murmured fretfully.

"For heaven's sake, Carrie," Lois said irritably, "you can't go listening to everything that Neelie says."

"That's good advice," agreed Clete. "That's a fine old colored lady and I know your mama was partial to her, but she's always going on about something or another. Best thing to do now is think we're going to find your daddy, and he's going to be safe and sound. More'n likely, he just got himself mixed up a little bit, but he knows how to take care of himself."

"We'll talk about it," Sam, Jr. said. "Try to think of where he might be."

"You do that. Maybe you'll come up with something," Clete replied. He added, "You know what I was thinking about this morning coming over here? I was remembering the time Mr. Sam stopped off at the house and told me to get out and hoe the grass from around some pecan trees he'd sold me. Said he didn't sell them to see them go to waste. That's a strong-minded man. He'll be all right."

The sons and daughters of Sam Peek thought of their father making a demand of Clete Walton. Their father was such a man. He had great nerve, great bravery.

Clete looked around the room. "By the way, where's James?" he asked.

For a moment no one spoke. Then Sam, Jr. said, "He went for a walk early this morning. I think he needed to be alone."

Clete wagged his head pontifically. "I can understand. You can tell them two is close. I saw them over in Hartwell not long ago, at the barber shop. The way James was watching out for him, I could tell they was close. Way it is sometimes with the baby of the family. They get attached, and it's hard to let go. Wish somebody thought that way of me."

James sat in a covering of trees on a knoll above Herman Morris' home. The morning air was still cold and he folded the collar of his thin windbreaker around his neck. He had walked for miles, rapidly, calming himself. He had not slept. He worried for his father, but there was also another image that he could not free from his mind — Herman Morris. He knew that if Herman Morris had fired his gun, he would have fired back, and there could have been a death. What he had done was foolish, and it was not his training to be foolish.

He saw a string of smoke curling from the chimney in Herman Morris' home. He thought: My God, the man must ache for his sons. His sons were worthless, made worthless by the lasting crush of poverty and by fear and by some primitive instinct for survival. I hope he understood me, James thought. I hope he knew that I was afraid for my father.

He watched as Herman Morris came out of his home and went to a stack of wood and gathered the wood in his arms. James could feel himself weeping.

TWENTY-TWO

Howard Cook watched in the rearview mirror of his car as the truck followed him, sputtering comically. He knew by the way the truck shook when it left his yard that Sam Peek was in third gear and had no intentions of changing. No wonder the gears were loose. But Sam Peek was an insistent man. Like Abraham leaving the land of Haran in the Old Testament, he was on a mission and would not let a few obstacles, such as first or second gear, stop him. Sam Peek was in his truck, sitting erect behind the steering wheel, elevated on his cushion, both hands clasped to the wheel as though driving at daredevil speed. Howard glanced at his speedometer. He was going thirty miles an hour. He thought: At this rate, it'll take more'n a half-hour to get there. Good thing we left when we did.

The pace did not bother Howard. He was doing something that made him feel good, something that seemed to matter. He had not had time to think it out, but Howard knew there was a lesson in Sam Peek. Howard believed in divine accidents, or interventions. Sam Peek had not wandered aimlessly over a mazemap of roads, passing dozens of deserted tenant farmhouses, to stop by chance, by coincidence, at the house of his childhood. No, not that. That would be too easy to understand, a statistical occurrence, like a lottery of numbers. The Lord had moved His invisible, beckoning finger in front of Sam Peek's eye, guiding him through the maze, commanding him to stop where he did. The Lord had directed Kenneth's attention to the car. The Lord had finally put Sam Peek and Howard Cook together, and there was a reason for it, a reason other than helping Sam Peek find his way to Madison.

From the rearview mirror, Howard saw that the truck ran more smoothly, with only a shimmer of vibration, but Sam Peek had not relaxed his grip. The white dog was beside him, sitting in the seat, the cap of her head and ears barely visible over the window. The dog's white fur looked like the sun's reflection on the window. Odd dog, Howard thought. Came from nowhere when Sam Peek called for her in his yard. He had been watching from the window of the living room with his wife because Sam Peek had told them the white dog would not show herself if anyone was in the yard with him, and they had agreed with looks of agreement between them that they would do as Sam Peek wished. "That dog ain't around here," he had whispered to Mildred. "We might find it up the road, but it ain't around here. Our dogs would've been barking." And then Sam Peek had clapped his hands once and called, "Come on, girl," and the dog had appeared beside him, rising up with her front feet on the bracing of the walker, and his wife had gasped in surprise.

Maybe the lesson the Lord had intended for him to learn was in the white dog, thought Howard. Maybe the dog was like the whale in the Jonah story, or like the lions with Daniel, or the doves of Noah's ark. Maybe the dog was the message and Sam Peek only the messenger.

Howard shrugged away with his shoulders the possibility of mystery in the white dog. He rubbed the palms of his hands over the arch of the steering wheel. He was letting his imagination get the best of him. The Lord had delivered Sam Peek to him because the Lord knew he would help Sam Peek. It was that simple. No need to read anything else into it, like some preachers he knew, preachers who would take the simplest Bible verse — clear and lovely as the poetry of a nursery rhyme — and make of it a farfetched tale of doom, as vivid as Armageddon. Howard did not like such preachers. They feasted on the stench of fear, like the predator buzzard circling the rising odor of a killed, decaying animal. Howard had been a good neighbor, a good Samaritan. Nothing more. But that was enough in the Lord's asking. He had taken an old man who was lost to his home, and he had fed him and given him rest, and his wife had put out a bath cloth and towel for a sponge-bath, and she had pressed the old man's suit shirt, and now he was delivering that old man to the place he wanted to go. The Lord must be pleased, he thought.

He did not know why Howard Cook insisted on driving so fast, speeding along almost as recklessly as the other cars and trucks that shot past them in a blur of colored metal. If I'd of wanted to fly, I'd of taken an airplane, he thought irritably. No sense in going so fast. Howard Cook was a good man, but he was like Noah and Holman when it came to driving a vehicle. Noah and Holman drove like madmen. Noah and Holman never thought about looking at things on the side of the road, only about getting to where they were going. He liked to look. There were things to be seen on the side of the road that were worth remembering — like the Apalachee River they had crossed a mile or two back. As a young man at Madison A&M, he had often fished the Apalachee with Marshall Harris, bringing back strings of catfish for the farm workers to cook in a large black frypan balanced on the rock wall of an outdoor fire. Once he had found the shards of Indian pottery in the mudsand of the river, and a history professor from the school had delivered a lecture on Indians native to the area. Such things were worth remembering.

The truck hummed in a steady tremble running from the steering wheel into his hands and arms. He worried that something might suddenly fly off the truck or from beneath its rusting hood, and the truck would be as crippled as he was, or it would die in the road, steam spewing from its mechanical organs like a human soul passing into the ether of heaven. He looked at the speedometer. Great God Almighty, he thought. Howard Cook was pushing forty miles an hour. No need to be going so fast.

He saw Howard's car slow in front of him and then saw the winking of the left blinker light. Howard had said they would make a hard left at a church and then turn quickly back to the right under a railroad trestle. He saw the church on the left of the road. Howard's car slowed to a stop and then made the turn. He hesitated, watching for traffic. "It's a hard turn," he remembered Howard saying. "You have to be careful about traffic coming at you. There's a curve there." He did not see any cars or trucks, and he pushed on the accelerator and the truck jerked forward in slow, laboring spurts and he guided it behind Howard's car, following Howard in the right turn on the road beneath the railroad trestle. He did not see Howard Cook shaking his head in disbelief, and he did not hear Howard Cook offering a prayer of gratitude to God for the braking power of the tractor-trailer truck that had slowed miraculously in time to allow Sam Peek's sputtering truck to cross in front of it.

"Thank you, Jesus," Howard said with a dry mouth.

The landmarks leading into Madison were no longer familiar to him, but still he knew he was nearing the land he had farmed at the school of his youth. He knew intuitively, like birds with the unerring radar of familiarity returning to distant places, following memories so splendid they could not be resisted. He slowed his truck and, ahead of him, Howard Cook slowed his car. "We're almost there, girl," he said to White Dog. The dog looked at him and whimpered. "I know that land over there. I used to plow that land."

In the distance he saw the rust-red brick of buildings off to his right. "Up there," he said, "that's where the school used to be. They tore it down. Put up a high school. Don't know why they tore it down, but they did."

Howard looked at the speedometer on his car. Twenty miles per hour. He knew that Sam Peek had recognized, at last, where he was. He glanced at his watch. It was eleven-thirty. Sam Peek had said the lunch was at twelve. We made it in time, he thought. He would pull off at the road leading to Morgan County High School and bid farewell to Sam Peek, then he would drive into town on his pretension of business and wait a few minutes before driving back to his home. And he would do one other thing: he would call Sam Peek's family in Hart County and tell them what had happened and advise his preacher sons to come for their father. If Sam Peek had gotten lost coming to Madison, he would get lost going home.

"Glad I got to know you, Mr. Peek," Howard said to him, shaking his hand through the opened door of the truck. "Hope you enjoy the reunion. You ever get back down this way, we'd be glad to have you stop in."

"Wish you'd let me pay you," Sam Peek said. "You and your wife went out of your way helping me out."

"No sir," Howard said pleasantly. "Couldn't take nothing for what little we done. Just glad we was there."

"So was I," he said. "You come up to Hart County, we'll repay you for the kindness."

"Maybe we'll do that someday," Howard replied. "Not far away. Maybe I'll come up there and get me a couple of them trees you was telling us about. Wouldn't mind having me some pear trees."

"You let me know, and I'll have them up and heeled in for you," he said. "Pick out the best I got." He did not have pear trees, but he would order them from another nursery and pretend that he grew them.

"I'll do that. You take care of yourself. You need anything, you have somebody call Howard Cook. I'm in the book."

"I appreciate it," he said. He shook hands again with Howard and watched him get into his car and drive off. He would write in his journal of Howard and he would send a check to Howard's church. He would do it in Cora's memory.

He drove his truck down the short road leading from the highway to the school and turned into the middle driveway and parked beside a flagpole, across from the row of cars already there. The cars gleamed from being washed clean and waxed and his truck, among them, would be an eyesore, an embarrassment. He felt displaced. He sat in the high cab of his truck, rubbing his dog at the neck, looking at the school and the row of gleaming cars. He had traveled a day and a half to get there, and now he was uncomfortable. No one else had arrived in an old junk-heap of a truck and no one else would have a dog with them. The dog moved restlessly from his hand and looked over the edge of the window to the outside.

"Guess maybe you want to get out and run," he said to the dog. "In a minute. In a minute, maybe. Let's just sit here for a little while."

Another car — white, long as a limousine — moved down the driveway and parked beside the other cars. A woman — young, energetic, lithe — got out of the car from the driver's seat and hurried to open the passenger's door. A frail, bent man emerged hesitantly from the car. He wore a light blue suit. His white hair fluttered in the easy breeze. He was thin, fragile — so delicately fragile a strong hand might shatter him. He had a cane, and he slipped forward a few steps on the walkway, scraping forward, never lifting his feet, and then he stopped and propped both hands on the nob of the cane. He turned slowly in a half-circle and looked around, as though looking for something he could remember. The woman stood near him, her hands lifted, ready to catch and steady him. She laughed gaily and said something to the man.

Who could that be? he wondered. Who could be that old and come back for the reunion? He tried to remember a body that would match the frail, bent man, tried to have the man stand straight and young and powerful in his imagination, but he could not. Lonice Carswell? Lonice had had blond hair, and it was always wild on his head, as though he had been running in a windstorm, but Lonice was dead. Or was he?

He watched the man and the woman — the man's granddaughter, he reasoned — make their way up the walkway and into the building, the woman chattering cheerfully, directing her fragile grandfather, on guard against a stumble that would send him crashing to the ground, shattering him. My God, he thought, are we that old? Are we all that old? He thought of one of his own granddaughters, one who had always tugged at him for attention. If he had asked, she would have driven him in her car to the reunion and she could have walked with him into the building, holding the door for him, watching that he might stumble.

The door to the building opened, and a woman, regally dressed, her grey-blue hair swirled in a crown on her head, stepped outside. He knew her instantly: Martha Dunaway Kerr. She was holding a paper. She stood for a moment, looking at the gleaming, parked cars. She glanced once toward his truck, then looked away and turned and went back inside the building. He wondered if she had come outside, looking for him. Martha Dunaway Kerr. Once, after his engagement to Cora had been announced, Martha said to him, blithely, "Why, Sam, didn't you know? I've had my sights on you all this time, and now you go off and get yourself caught by another woman." She had laughed and hugged him quickly and then danced away, calling to someone else.

"Let's go," he said to the dog. "I'll take you some place you can run." He pushed the starter pedal and pulled the gearshift down and felt it click and he eased his left foot (his bad leg) up from the clutch and the truck pulled away smoothly. "Got the right gear," he mumbled.

The road was still there, as it had been when he was first a student and then superintendent of the farm at Madison A&M. The road led to the creek where he had proposed to Cora. Now there were pastures and pine tree stands along the road, where fields had been, where he had planted and harvested corn and wheat and cotton, but he knew the road, and the truck turned obediently under his hand until he came to the creek.

A pasture pushed up to the edge of hardwood trees that lined the creekbank, and he sat in his truck with the motor idling and carefully studied the pasture and trees. "Used to be a wagon path somewhere," he said absently. "Maybe we can drive down it if it's still there."

He did not see the wagon path, but he did see a drop-down gate in the barbed wire fence. A large culvert had been placed in the gully to bridge crossing vehicles. He eased the truck over the culvert and got out and hobbled on his walker to the fence and released the drop-down gate. Then he got back into his truck and drove into the pasture. He did not worry about resetting the gate. He had not seen any cattle, and the only reason to have a fence would be cattle. And he did not think that he was trespassing. No one knew the land he was on as intimately as he had known it.

The pasture land had been packed hard by the summer's heat and it was easy to drive over. He followed the graceful, curving line of trees until he came to a place that veered close to the water and he could see through the trees the muscle of granite that bulged from the ground, and he knew he was where he wanted to be. He stopped the truck and got out. The sun's warmth felt good on his back. "Come on, girl," he said to White Dog. The dog slipped from the truck. "Go run, girl. Go run."

It was past twelve o'clock. The reunion lunch was being served at Morgan County High School, and Martha Dunaway Kerr was presiding with dignity over the sparse gathering of old people, but he was glad he was not among them. If Cora had lived,

155

if Cora had been with him, it would have mattered; without her, it did not.

He took his journal from the suitcase and tucked it inside his shirt and worked his way cautiously into the woods and to the shade of the pines. He found the place he had been with Cora, where he could see the water splitting over the shoals. The smell of the water and the moss pads near the water was as sweet as it had been sixty years earlier. He raked together a seat of the needles with his foot and lowered himself with his walker, stretching his bad leg straight. He opened his journal and removed the picture of Cora and Marshall Harris and looked at it for a long time. Then he replaced it and took his pen and began to write in his unsteady hand:

> Today is the reunion and I did not go. I am at a place where I asked
> Cora to marry me 57 years ago. It is the place I wanted to be. I
> always liked it here. I wish Cora could be with me but the
> Almighty had different plans for her. We should have come back
> here earlier, when we could. I still remember the day when we
> walked across the fields and came down here. It was the best day
> of my life. I wish I could live it over again, but I can't. Having
> it to remember is the best I can do. I am tired, not having slept
> well in my truck last night. A preacher, Howard Cook, and his
> family helped me out or I wouldn't be here now. I guess I will
> drive back home today, but if it starts to get dark I will stop some
> where and find me a room to sleep in. I guess my children know
> by now that I did not go to see Neal Lewis and they are worried
> about me. I'm sure they'll keep an eye on me from now on. My
> white dog is running in the woods. She likes this place as much
> as I do.

The writing had made his hand cramp, and the lulling rush of the water had made him sleepy, but he knew he could not sleep. He looked at his watch. He had been there for more than an hour. He called to his dog, "Come on, girl. Come on." The dog raced to him quickly and lay beside him and pushed her head into his lap. "Can't rest now," he said, stroking the dog's head. "We got to be going back. We got a long way to drive."

He stood at the creekbank for a long time, watching the water spinning across the shoals. He would never again see this place, and he wanted the last vision of it locked securely in his memory. He then drove back through the pasture and reset the drop-gate at the fence and drove to the highway leading into Madison. He looked at his watch again. It was past two o'clock. He turned right and drove toward the school.

There were no cars at the school, and he turned his truck into the driveway and parked again on the roadside and got out. "Stay in the truck," he said to his dog. "I won't be long." He took his walker and crossed the street and followed the walkway to the building where he had seen Martha Dunaway Kerr. To his surprise, the door was unlocked, and he went inside. It was not the building of his youth, and walking inside it was a curious, unsettling experience. He did not know why he was there or what he should be looking for — if anything — but being there seemed imperative, as though nothing else would end the odyssey of foolishness that had preoccupied him for weeks.

He followed the corridor to a door leading into the school's cafeteria, and he pushed open the door and stepped inside. The decorations for the reunion lunch were still there — balloons, crepe paper streamers, the banner he had expected. The banner read: Madison A&M Reunion. The banner's purple and gold colors were faded. It had been used many times. His eyes scanned the empty room. It didn't last long, he thought. Sixty years to talk over, and done with in two hours. But maybe they hadn't come to talk over sixty years. Maybe they had come, as he had, to look for something that no longer existed.

He pivoted on his walker back through the door and began to move back down the hallway. His head was down and he did not see her approaching him.

"Sam?" she said. "Sam Peek?"

He stopped and looked up.

"It's me. Martha."

TWENTY-THREE

"If I hadn't forgotten my papers and had to come back for them, I'd have missed you," Martha Dunaway Kerr was saying again to him. She had insisted on talking and had guided him back into the cafeteria and to a table, and now she was sitting close to him, her voice clear and lively and her face as animated as it had been when she was a girl.

"I can't believe your granddaughter's car broke down on the way here," she said, touching his hands with hers, removing them, touching them again. "What a day for that to happen. I'm so sorry, Sam. Everybody was asking about you. I told them you were coming, that I'd gotten your registration card and money, but something must have happened."

"It took a while to get the car started again," he lied. "She dropped me off here and went on to town to see about it. Just thought I'd walk around the place and look it over."

"But you're staying for tonight, aren't you?"

He shook his head. "My granddaughter has to be back at her home tomorrow. She lives in Atlanta."

"But, Sam, this is a special time," Martha Dunaway Kerr protested. Her voice softened. "It may be the last time. Nobody talked about having another one."

"Wish I could stay, Martha, but I can't," he said. "I was headed outside to wait for my granddaughter. We have to get back."

"All right, I won't argue," she said, "but tell me about you. Cora? Is she —?"

"Passed away earlier this year," he replied simply. "She was looking forward to coming down for the reunion."

"How —?"

"Heart attack. Took her quick. I'm grateful for that."

Martha Dunaway Kerr's face furrowed in sadness. "My husband — David — had cancer. Took months before he died. He suffered badly. I'd like to go like Cora. I'd like for it to be swift and merciful."

He did not reply. He looked into Martha Dunaway Kerr's face. Her eyes were still magnificently blue and clear.

"I remember Cora so well," she said suddenly, her voice brightening. "She was so beautiful. The girls always talked about that — how pretty she was. And I can tell you, Sam, there were a good number of them who envied her when she started seeing you." She laughed girlishly. "For a while, until I met David, I was among them." She touched his hands again. "You were a handsome thing, Sam Peek. Shy as the day is long, but handsome. I used to watch you working out in the fields, and I knew you'd become somebody special, and you have, Sam. You have."

"Special?" he said in surprise. "Don't know how you get that."

"Good heavens, Sam, you've been written up lots of times. I subscribe to a number of horticultural journals, and I used to read about you all the time. Quotes from Sam Peek. Very profound. You're one of the smartest men in the south when it comes to trees. Do you know that I have some of your trees in my yard?"

"How?" he asked.

"I sent for them. Told the man to tell you they were for me, but when I asked him about it later, he said he'd forgotten to say anything. I think he was afraid of getting the wrong thing and was worried what I'd say. I started to write, but I didn't. I wasn't sure you'd remember who Martha Dunaway was."

"Didn't know about that," he told her. "Sorry he didn't say anything. I would have remembered you. Would have made sure you had the best in the field. Hope the ones you got did all right."

"They're beautiful. They're pecan trees, that special variety you propagated. I sit out under them all the time in the summer. It's so cool out under those trees."

"I've sort of retired from all of that," he said quietly.

"Well, of course you have. You should have," she said. "But you made a name for yourself before you did. And your boys, your preacher sons, they've become quite famous, I understand."

He thought of Howard Cook. He wondered if Martha Dunaway Kerr knew Howard. "The boys have done all right," he said. "The girls, too. We had some good children. Mostly Cora's doing."

"I — I never had children," she said. "Sometimes I regret that. David wanted them badly, but we couldn't have them. So you, see, Sam, you're fortunate you didn't get caught by me. You wouldn't have had your wonderful children."

He did not know what to say. He looked away from her face.

"Oh, but don't go feeling sorry for me, Sam," she said quickly. "We had a good life together. Got to travel around and see things. And I've loved Madison. Don't know of any other place on the earth I'd rather be, and I've seen them all, from Europe to Asia. There's something timeless about this place, though. It's still as beautiful as it used to be."

"It's changed a lot," he said. "Like the school. When they tore down the buildings, it changed what I remember."

Martha Dunaway Kerr nodded and closed her eyes, as though framing a portrait in her mind. "I fought against that, Sam," she said. She opened her eyes. "I did everything I could to stop that from happening, but that was a long time ago and nobody listened to women in those days." She smiled. "Not that they do much now."

"How many people showed up for the lunch?" he asked.

She patted his hand again. "Not many. Eleven, counting me. You would have been twelve. But you did show up, didn't you? Just a little late, but you're here, and you count. So, twelve showed up. Twelve came back. For sixty years, that's not bad, is it?"

He wanted to ask about the frail, bent man with the white hair, but knew that he couldn't. "It's more'n I thought would be here," he said.

"So many are dead, Sam. So many. But that's to be expected, isn't it? We're in our eighties now. I don't expect to live much longer, Sam. Do you?"

"Always thought I'd make it to a hundred," he replied lightly, "but that was when I was fifty. No, not much longer now."

"Does it scare you, Sam?"

"Sometimes. Not much, though."

"Me, either." She took his hands and held them. Her hands were warm on his. "Oh, there are days when I want to blink my eyes and have it all turned back, back to when we were children. I want to run again and dance and do all those things that I loved doing, but I know it's not to be. Know what I do, Sam? I get out my albums, with all the pictures, and I look at them and pretend that somebody just took that picture yesterday. It makes me feel all young again. And then I look in the mirror, or at my hands . . ." She lifted her hands from his hands and looked at them, at the rows of bone beneath the pale, thin skin. "I look at my hands and know how foolish I've been," she whispered.

He reached for her hands and held them. She was still a child, he thought. This remarkable, dignified woman was still a child. A moist film filled in her clear, blue eyes.

"I'm glad I had a chance to see you, Martha," he said.

She nodded and smiled, then she stood. "I think I have to go along, Sam," she said bravely. "There's things to be done before tonight. Everybody's on the tour now. Some young people from the Chamber of Commerce are guiding them."

He pulled himself up on his walker. "I'll walk out with you," he said.

"I'd like that."

They walked together, without speaking, out of the cafeteria, down the hallway and out to the front of the building.

"Are you sure your granddaughter's coming back soon?" Martha Dunaway Kerr asked. "There's nobody else around, except maybe the janitor. That must be his truck over there."

He looked at his truck. He could see White Dog staring at him from the window. "She'll be by," he said. "I'll just wait here."

"Goodbye, Sam," Martha Dunaway Kerr said. "I don't suppose we'll see each other again."

"We could," he said. "Maybe we'll both make it to a hundred. We do, we'll have a reunion, just the two of us."

She leaned across his walker and hugged him quickly, then walked away to her car.

He waited until Martha Dunaway Kerr's car was out of sight and he was confident that she would not return. Then he got into his truck and drove away without looking back at the school he did not know. He said to White Dog, "We got a long way to go."

He was on the road, driving back toward Greensboro, when he heard the horn of the car behind him. He slowed and looked into the rearview mirror. He could see arms waving from the car and then the car pulled beside him and he looked out of his window to see James pointing for him to pull over to the side of the road.

"Well, girl, they found us," he said to White Dog. "I guess I'm glad." He guided his truck to a jolting stop.

TWENTY-FOUR

He did not tolerate questions about his unannounced trip to Madison. He said, indignantly, "I made up my mind to go at the last minute. I can go see Neal Lewis anytime I want to, but that was the last reunion for us. Your mama wanted to go; told me that before she died. I made up my mind that's what I'd do, and I went."

The explantation that Neal Lewis knew nothing about a planned visit with him was a weak argument. "Neal's getting old," he said flatly. "Maybe he forgot." The way he said it — defensively, angrily — made his children wonder: Was it Neal who had forgotten or was it their father?

"Don't know why you worried to begin with," he said. "I had my dog with me. My dog takes care of me."

"Babies," Neelie said privately to Kate and Carrie, "that dog wadn't doing nothing. That dog was what took Mr. Sam off. That dog a ghost dog. You got to keep a watch on Mr. Sam when he with that dog. He be gone again."

But he did not, again, go away alone. He permitted his daughters and sons and their husbands and wives and his grandchildren to drive him for his needs — his haircuts and groceries and banking business. And sometimes they drove him to funerals, to sit among the depleting gathering of men in the rocking chairs on the front porches of funeral parlors.

"Another one gone," the men always said matter-of-factly, and then they would praise the departed by reciting (and embellishing) some small, special story out of memory. The dead had been good, or the dead had been mischievous or thrifty or strong or shy or outrageous or brave or jovial or any of countless other attributes that, given forgiveness for shortcomings, made for a likeable person. That was the common agreement among them: the dead had been likeable, and in their front-porch, rocking-chair eulogies, the men who remained — waiting their turn to be likeable — momentarily elevated the deceased to a rare, but impermanent history.

Ira Carter.

Tom Mabry.

One by one they died, and he attended their funerals.

Oscar Beatenbo.

Herman Dudley.

Their names were read on the Obituary Column of the Air by a solemn-voiced announcer as organ music sang softly in the background, and he recorded their names dutifully in his journal.

Pete Mullinax.

Neal Lewis.

"Won't be needing these rockers much longer. Won't be nobody here to sit in them."

"Great God Almighty, they ain't but a handful of us left."

"Won't be none of us before long."

"That's the truth."

He went to the funerals and joined in the eulogies that found the deceased likeable, but only one death greatly affected him — Neelie's. When Neelie died, three years after his trip to Madison, he wept painfully. He ordered a majestic headstone for Neelie in the names of his children.

As the months became years (blurringly swift), he became interested in, and then obsessed with, the genealogy of his family and of his wife's family, and he spent many hours each week writing letters, gathering information that he carefully structured in the tree-shape of matings and progeny. Piece by piece, he put the tree together, going from the thick, name-heavy bottom limbs upward and as he went upward on his paper tree, he went backward in time and place — from Georgia to the Carolinas, from the Carolinas to Virginia, from Virginia to Pennsylvania, from Pennsylvania to England and Ireland. He found among his ancestors (and hers) laborers and politicians, preachers and trappers, carpenters, silversmiths, thieves, farmers, soldiers, journalists, teachers. With each discovery he felt less lonely.

And he began to do one other thing that he had seldom done: he began to talk freely with his children of his own childhood, and they were amazed at the man who was their father.

"Funny, when Mama was alive, Daddy never said much," Carrie remarked to Kate. "Now he talks all the time. James said he's always told him stories, but I don't know that he's ever said much to the rest of us."

"I think James is special to him, James being the youngest," Kate said. "Wonder how much of it's true? Old people get to the point where they make things up and swear they happened, especially when there's nobody else around to call their hand on it. I heard somebody talking about that on television. Art Linkletter, maybe."

"Good Lord, Kate, don't get started again," exclaimed Carrie. "Nothing's wrong with Daddy's mind. It's clear as a bell."

"I don't know," Kate said. "Did you ever hear Mama talk about him having a sister who died of the smallpox plague and was buried in a common grave with lots of other people?"

"No, but he said he did," Carrie argued. "And that's good enough for me. Just because he never talked about it before, doesn't mean it didn't happen."

"That was our aunt, Carrie," Kate said pitifully. "We don't even know where to take flowers."

His daughters and sons visited often with him, bringing their children and their grandchildren to embrace him. The smaller ones sat on his lap, with warnings of injury to his hip, and he fed them bits of soft peppermint candy that he kept in a sealed jar, pushed to the back of his roll-top desk. He did not know all of his grandchildren or great-grandchildren, but he pretended that he did. He gave them silver dollars for accomplishments and sent them birthday cards that he selected from the card rack in the drugstore (reminded by Kate or Carrie of their names and birthdates). When they left him after their visits, he sat quietly in his chair, hearing their echoes. Their echoes were noisy. Their echoes lasted as long as he wished to hear them.

He visited regularly at her grave—Cora's grave—and at the grave of his oldest son. It was peaceful in the cemetery.

White Dog was with him. Always with him. At night, White Dog curled at the bottom of his bed. No one else touched White Dog.

He wrote in his journal—brief, daily footnotes of brief, daily occurrences.

— Received the seed catalogue I ordered. I won't send off for any seed, but I like looking at the pictures of flowers.

— Lois and Tabor came by today to show me their new car. It is a Ford.

— This afternoon I took a nap and dreamed of some gypsies that came by the house forty years ago. Don't know why I had such a dream.

— Today is Mother's Day. I put some flowers in the church in Cora's memory.

— A man from New York stopped by to see if I had some trees for sale. He said his father had bought trees from me. I told him I was retired, but it was not the right time to be putting out trees, being the middle of July and the sap running. When he left I remembered the time James sold a man from New York four stalks of cotton for a dollar apiece, telling the man it was a rare southern plant and not to worry if it wilted a few miles up the road. I had to spank James for that, but I knew I'd never have to worry about him making a living.

— It rained all day and it was cold. I had to turn on the heater for a little while. White Dog and I stayed inside.

— Kate and Carrie have been out today cleaning the house before Alma and Lois show up this weekend to clean it. Said they didn't want it to be such a mess. I will never understand my daughters.

— One of Neelie's grandsons came by today to bring me some tenderloin from a hog killing. He is a handsome, light-skinned boy, well-mannered like all of Neelie's grandchildren. She taught them to be proper and all of them are making a good life. I still miss Neelie. The tenderloin was the best I've had in a long time.

— My hip hurt today. Except to feed White Dog and get a bite for myself, I have stayed in my chair.

— Listened to a radio preacher shouting his head off about the end of the world and asking for money to keep going until then. He said the world was going to end on March 10, 1979. I think I'll send him a check and postdate it March 11.

In late spring of 1980, he was watching television, and the program was about the symptoms of cancer, and he knew instantly that he was dying.

He sat for a long time after the program was over, his eyes closed, and tried to feel the nibbling of the cancer's voracious feeding inside him. It was there, its wide, acid mouth devouring the succulent, tender-sweet flesh of his body. He knew it was there — the mutant cannibal; he could feel it moving in him.

I will not die quickly, he thought. Not like Cora. There will not be a time bomb erupting in my heart like an unexpected suicide. No, I will not die quickly.

He called for White Dog, and the dog trotted to his chair and nuzzled her face into his hand.

"I'm going to hurt, girl," he said quietly to his dog.

His journal entry that night was:

I realized tonight that I have cancer and am dying from it. I do not know how long it will take for the cancer to kill me, but I know it will be painful. I hope the Almighty will give me the strength to stand up to the pain and not make me much of a burden on my children. I would like to die fast, like Cora died, but I do not believe that will happen. I will die like Hattie Lewis died, wasting away until there is nothing else to do but die. I know I am right about this, but tomorrow I will make an appointment with the doctor. If I am lucky, I will be with Cora and Thomas before too much longer.

Three days later a doctor in Athens confirmed what he already knew.

"How long do you think I have?" he asked matter-of-factly.

"Hard to say, Mr. Peek," the doctor said in a tired, sad voice. "A few months. Maybe a year."

"I appreciate you telling me straight-out," he said to the doctor.

The doctor nodded. The doctor had seen many people die,

had too many times been the messenger, the announcer, of gloom, and the task always left him with a sour taste in his mouth, as though the words were bitter fruit.

"A lot of what happens will be up to you," the doctor said. "I don't know why — I don't think anybody does — but the way a person thinks and acts has a lot to do with their health. I've known people with milder cases of cancer than you've got, Mr. Peek, and they've walked out of here and were buried in less than a month. Not because the cancer killed them, no matter what we put on the death certificate. What killed them was their own determination. They wanted to die, and they did. They didn't have to, not that fast. I hope you do the opposite, Mr. Peek. I hope you fight it with everything you've got in you."

"I used to think I'd live to be a hundred," he said absently. The doctor stood at his desk. He picked up the charts before him and glanced at them. He said, "You know, if it wasn't for the cancer, you would. You're the healthiest man I've ever examined at your age. You've got the heart of a thirty-year-old man. Yes, I think you would have made it."

"I just hope I don't get to be a burden," he said.

"You're lucky," the doctor told him. "You've got a good family. They'll share what needs to be done. Don't think about being a burden. I promise you, they'll want to take care of you." The doctor paused, then said, "Do you want me to tell your daughters, the ones that came with you?"

He thought of Kate and Carrie waiting anxiously outside the doctor's office. They would become hysterical. Best not to let them know. Not now. He would tell James and let James keep the secret until it had to be known. Once he had kept such a secret for James — when James went to southeast Asia before the Vietnam war, when everyone thought he was in Hawaii, in a soft, sunlit Army paradise (all his letters were postmarked Hawaii), but he was not; he was in Thailand, where war simmered like a volatile temper. James would know the value of keeping a secret.

"No," he said to the doctor. "Don't tell them. Not yet. I'd rather do it in my own way."

"Whatever you wish, Mr. Peek. You understand they'll have to know before long."

"I understand," he said.

That night he called James and said to him, "Son, I need you."

"All right, Daddy," James replied. "I'll be there in three hours."

TWENTY-FIVE

James would keep his father's secret for two months and then he would beg to be released from his commitment.

"I know how I'd feel if I was one of the others, Daddy," he said to his father. "I'd want to know. I'd want to have some time to take it all in."

"All right, son," he agreed. "I guess it's time. I can't keep putting it off."

"Do you want me to tell them?" James asked.

"It's all right with me."

His family responded as he knew they would. His daughters swirled around him, with large, frightened eyes, busying themselves in his house, trying to talk cheerfully, but failing. His sons were quiet, serious. Sometimes his sons would ask if he needed anything taken care of that might be unpleasant, some preparation for his dying like wills or final wishes. He insisted that his children not begin their hovering until it was necessary.

"I'm not helpless," he said to them. "Maybe I'll get that way, but I'm not now. Having people coming in every few minutes makes me tired. Can't do what I want to do, when I want to do it."

"We just don't want you to be alone, Daddy," his children said.

"I'm not alone," he argued. "I've got my dog."

And he knew what his children were saying among themselves.

"His dog. Seems like that's all he cares about. Maybe Neelie was right about that dog. Maybe she's got a spell on him. Never saw him that crazy about any animal before."

"It's just a dog."

"That's all it is. Nothing but a dog."

"You wouldn't say that if you lived around here," Kate vowed. "Would they, Carrie?"

"Sometimes it's scary," Carrie reported in a hushed voice. "You'd think we could at least touch her after all these years, but we can't. Nobody can. And you don't ever see any other dogs around her. Never. Don't ever hear them bark, or anything."

"Never," emphasized Kate.

They were saying among themselves that only White Dog seemed to matter. He knew what they were saying, but they did not understand.

The cancer moved through him, feasting.

In the summer, in the heat of the summer, he became weak and did not often leave his house and the whirling blades of the fan aimed at his armchair. He ate sparingly, not caring for the food, even when it was food that he had enjoyed. "No need for so much food," he said to his children. "Not doing anything. No need to eat much unless I'm working."

He could not work. He did not go into his plot of pecan trees to pull away the grass and the grass matted the ground. He could see it from the kitchen window. That's done with, he thought. I won't work the trees again. He took the last order book that he had used and looked up the name of the person who purchased the last tree he would ever sell, and then he recorded that man's name in his journal.

> Dorsey Pilgreen from Anderson, South Carolina, bought two pecan trees from me on April 11. They are the last trees I sold, out of thousands over the years.

The cancer feasted.

On a Sunday in the autumn he went with Lois and Tabor for a drive into the north Georgia mountains to see the leaves of the hardwoods. The leaves were brilliantly colored — reds and golds dripping from limbs like hot lava spills — and he asked Tabor to stop at a pulloff near a path leading into the woods.

"Need to stretch a minute," he said as excuse.

"I do, too," Tabor said as accommodation.

"Daddy, be careful," warned Lois. "There's some gravel out here."

He hobbled on his walker down the path, to a hanging tree limb of a tall pignut hickory. He reached up and touched a bright yellow leaf, took it between his fingers and caressed it. Then he pulled it from the tree and put it into his mouth and bit into it. The taste of the leaf — still pith-tender — was the taste of wood.

"All right," he said to Lois, "I'm ready to go home now."

That night, he told Kate, "I think it's time somebody started staying with me."

"All right, Daddy," Kate said softly. "We'll take care of it."

On Monday afternoon, Alma moved into the house with her suitcase, beginning the long-agreed schedule of care that would last until his death—a week-by-week alternating of his four daughters and, occasionally, his sons and daughters-in-law.

White Dog was in the room with him when Alma arrived. White Dog sat in a corner of the room, watching.

"It's the first time I've ever been this close to your dog, Daddy," Alma said. "You think she'll let me touch her?"

He shook his head. "Don't think so."

"She always runs away when we come in," Alma said. "Wonder why she didn't today?"

"Maybe she's tired, like I am," he answered.

"Well, you rest, Daddy. Whatever you need, I'm here." Alma left the room to put away the contents of her suitcase and White Dog crossed to him and placed her face in his lap.

"Not just the two of us any more," he said quietly to the dog. "Now we got to put up with people being around all the time."

The dog whined, rose up to the top brace of the walker beside his chair.

"You want out?" he said. "All right."

He pulled himself up on the walker and went to the kitchen door and opened it. The dog rose up again on the top brace and pushed her face into his hand, then dropped from the walker and trotted from the house.

He never again saw White Dog.

Each day he put out food, but the food was never eaten. He sat on the sideporch and watched the road and the fields, but he did not see the dog. He watched for circling buzzards, but there were none. He sent out his sons and his sons-in-law and his grandchildren to search for White Dog, but they returned to tell him they could not find her.

He wrote in his journal:

> *My dog of many years has disappeared. It happened on the day that my children moved back in to care for me. White Dog was a good companion, the best animal I ever had. I miss her but I do not think I will ever see her again. Maybe she got tired of me being sick. I, also, am tired of me being sick. The pain gets worse every day. I do not think it will be long now.*

Before he died, his body sipping from morphine to deaden the sharp-teeth gnawing of the mutant cannibal, he began to hallucinate. He saw Neelie at the bedroom window, and he laughed aloud and said to Alma and Lois, who were visiting at his bedside, "There's Neelie. Right there at the window. She's laughing, just laughing out loud. Got some more colored with her. But they're good people. They like me. They're good people." He talked with the memory of Marshall Harris, looking at Paul, believing Paul was Marshall. He believed Alma, was his wife, Cora. He mumbled incoherently about Hattie Lewis and Martha Dunaway Kerr.

His body withered.

He cried out for the barrel of a hypodermic needle, loaded with killing drops of instant mercy. "Why won't they let me die? I couldn't let my animals suffer like this. Why don't they take a gun and put me at ease?"

The cancer was ending its feast.

On the day before his death, he lay in his bed, his eyes clear, and he listened as James spoke calmly to him about trivial matters of family. James had taken pictures of the children and grandchildren.

"Thought you'd like to have them on the bedstand, Daddy," James said to him. "Soon as the prints come back, I'll have them framed."

He turned his eyes to James and he said, hoarsely, "You got a picture of my dog?"

"No, Daddy. I wish I did. I tried to take a picture one time, but I couldn't find her."

"She's gone," he said, his voice becoming firm.

"Yes sir. We keep looking for her, but we can't find her."

"She left."

"Yes sir."

"That was your mama, son."

James swallowed hard. "Who, Daddy?"

"White Dog. It was your mama come back to watch over me."

James did not reply. He took a damp bath cloth and wiped it across his father's forehead. He saw tears shining in his father's eyes.

"Your mama knew it was all right to go when you children came back," he said and he smiled. "I'm going to see her soon. I'll see my dog, too."

"Yes sir."

"Every night, White Dog was your mama."

"Mama?"

He nodded. He reached for his son's hand and held it. James could feel the skeleton of his father's fingers.

"It was your mama. Every night, she'd rest on the bed beside me. She looked like she did when she was a girl. She was pretty, son. She was a pretty girl."

James could barely speak. "You need to get some rest, Daddy."

"I'm all right, son. I feel good. I don't hurt."

"Do you want anything?"

He rolled his head on the pillow. His eyes were shining and there was an expression of gladness in his thin face. "You know where my dog is, son?"

"Where?"

"Up at the cemetery. She's waiting for me. I'm going there. You want to see her, go up there. Go up there in the morning, son. Right at sunup. She'll be there." He smiled happily and closed his eyes. His hand relaxed on his son's hand and he slept his morphine sleep.

He did not speak again. The cancer finished its feeding in the hollow, emaciated body.

On the day after his father was buried, James drove to the cemetery in the pink-blue glaze of dawn. The plot was still crowded with wreaths of flowers — flowers with bright, colorful faces and ribbon sashes — and the white, mica-sand covering of the ground was pockmarked where people had stood for the gravesite services and where chairs had been placed for the family.

James stood at the foot of the graves of his parents and his brother — a brother he had not known, a brother dead before his own birth — and stared at the shadowed sand mounds. Nothing was as permanent, he thought. Nothing. He turned and looked across the cemetery. His father had said the white dog would be there, to look for the white dog at sunrise. His father had said the white dog was his mother. He remembered Neelie's fearful warnings about ghost dogs. Maybe Neelie had said it often enough, and his father had subconsciously believed the stories.

His father was wrong. There was no white dog at the cemetery and there was nothing mysterious about the sunrise. It was only a quiet, pleasant time of the day. He tilted his head back and closed his eyes and breathed deeply, inhaling the perfume of the flowers and the clean, watery coolness of the air. Suddenly, a chill struck his neck and raced across his shoulders. He could feel his heart racing. He turned quickly, his eyes scanning the cemetery. Nothing. He began to walk slowly around the plot, searching. He could hear his father's voice. His father believed that White Dog would be at the cemetery.

The gauze curtain of morning was now lifted, and a soft brightness spilled through the trees. James walked into the plot, between the grave mounds of his mother and father, and he knelt. Then he saw them: across the chest of sand on the grave of Robert Samuel Peek, he saw the paw prints, prints so light they could have been made by air.

Author's Note

You will find in many novels a fine print disclaimer about the story, about the coincidence of similarity to real people and real events. It is a proclamation that fiction is fiction, regardless of its wellspring. This novel does not carry that disclaimer. It would be a lie. I have taken "To Dance With the White Dog" from truth — as I realized it — of my parents. There was a grand romance of life between them, and my father's loneliness following the death of my mother was a terrible experience for him. And there was a White Dog. And my father did believe White Dog was more than a stray. In this novel, I have changed names, numbers of children, and other facts. I did this for two reasons—dramatic intensity and detachment, both necessary in relating a personal memory to an unknown audience. I do not mean to offend the truth. I only wish to celebrate its spirit.

About the Author

Terry Kay grew up in Royston, Georgia, and now lives in Lilburn, Georgia. His previous works include the Emmy-winning screenplay, "Run Down the Rabbit," and the novels *The Year the Lights Came On* (1976), *After Eli* (which won the 1982 Best Fiction Award from the Georgia Council of Authors and Journalists), and *Dark Thirty* (1984). Both *After Eli* and *Dark Thirty* have been optioned for film production. Kay has also hosted "The Southern Voice," a public television series on Southern literature.